ROCK *Her*

RACHEL CROSS

Crimson Romance
New York London Toronto Sydney New Delhi

CRIMSON

Crimson Romance
An Imprint of Simon & Schuster, Inc.
1230 Avenue of the Americas
New York, NY 10020

ISBN 978-1-4405-6899-2
ISBN 978-1-4405-6900-5 (ebook)

Dedication

For Chris
&
In loving memory of Doc and Effie

Acknowledgments

Many, many thanks to my beta readers, critiquers and enthusiasts: A.B. Clarke, Lee-Ann, Allyson, Debi O., Jennifer G, Brona, Ketty, Nicola, Michelle Josette, Joey, Al, Cristen, Kirsten, Tamara, Kristi, and Camille.

Heartfelt thanks to my wonderful Crimson Romance editors: Jennifer Lawler, Julie Sturgeon, and Ashley Myers.

Finally, to sisters and friends who have supported and loved me through *all* of my journeys, thank you.

Chapter 1

She's okay, Mom.

As her feet pounded out a rhythm on the hard packed sand, her mother's tarnished locket with its shiny new chain bounced on her chest. She held it briefly before sliding it back under her shirt.

Kate took the first mile slowly, warming up her legs as she ran the sloping path from her two-bedroom guesthouse to Mar Vista Beach. The surf was small. Nevertheless, two surfers were offshore trying to catch waves. Her only other company was a beachcomber or runner, barely visible in the distance. Heading south to the point break, she picked up her pace.

All those years making meals for two, checking homework, cheering Emma on in life and sports; it all came to an abrupt end when Kate put Emma on the plane four weeks ago. Her sister, attending college three thousand miles away. Was it possible to have empty-nest syndrome at twenty-five?

The dog—Zack, according to his collar—was a welcome and familiar sight at this beach. While his owner surfed the break, Zack waited patiently with his tennis ball. Kate bent to pick up the soggy ball and pitched it into the waves. Zack retrieved it as she continued running. He chased her for a few steps, hopeful.

Some mornings Kate was so lost in her thoughts she wouldn't have noticed if her path took her straight through a nude sunbathing area. But today everything distracted her, the blue gray of the Pacific, the pelicans diving in the wide gap between the two surfers waiting for waves, and the beauty of home.

Kate watched one of the surfers, Zack's owner. She'd seen him numerous times on her runs, sitting, his board perfectly angled to see the incoming waves. Fall was calm, unlike winter when storms could bring waves twenty feet high to this part of the California coast. Growing up in Cielito, almost everyone surfed something at some point. Longboard, shortboard, bodyboard, stand up paddleboard—there was a board for everyone. She had spent countless hours surfing, swimming, and bodyboarding at this very beach. Now? Despite the heat her run generated, she gave a small shiver. The ocean was cold, even with a wetsuit. She'd take a heated swimming pool any day over that sixty-degree water.

The same two surfers were still in their spots as she made her way back down the beach. She threw the ball for Zack again and lifted a hand to his owner. He sat on his board waiting for the next set of waves, but he raised a hand in return.

She looked out to the other surfer, some fifty yards from Zack's owner. Not there. Odd. He was there a second ago; his board was still there. She picked up her pace, staring intently at the space where the surfer should've been. Nothing. No one on the beach either. What the hell? Why was his surfboard still sitting, fins up, as if anchored...

Oh no. Oh my God.

Functioning solely on adrenaline, she raced to the water, barely pausing to toe off her shoes in the icy surf before running into the sea. Numb within seconds from the cold, she took one deep breath and plunged under the first breaking wave.

The sea was calm as she struck out for the board with a frantic freestyle stroke. Panic lent her speed. She reached the surfboard in moments. She took another deep breath—not easy since exhaustion from the run, coupled with the cold Pacific, left her damn near hyperventilating.

She dove into the murky water under the board, hands searching for and finding the flexible rubber tube, the leash, which normally attached a surfer to his board. She hoped and prayed it was still attached. She yanked it. Heavy. She followed the leash down, deeper until icy flesh brushed her fingers. His ankle. *Thank God.*

She grabbed for him, barely able to see his black clad body in the dark water. She ran her hands up his ankle, past his leg and hip, until she reached his chest. She wrapped one arm under his wetsuit-covered armpit, then kicked with all her strength, finally breaking the surface.

Gasping for breath, legs pumping, she struggled to pull the unconscious man's limp head out of the water. *He weighs a ton!*

She looked up to see the other surfer, Zack's owner, in front of her. He rolled off his board without a word, turned it upside down, fins up, draped the man's arms over the board, and with considerable exertion, levered it up and over. The board flipped, distributing the unconscious man's torso onto the middle of the board. He unleashed the man from his shorter inverted surfboard, which pitched on the waves. With the board in front of him, he started for shore, Kate in his wake. The dark-haired man fought the beach break, barely managing to keep the board upright. He grunted as he dragged the drowning victim off the board, then turned him face up, just beyond the water's edge. Kate all but crawled out of the water on his heels. Muscles cramped from the cold, she hobbled over to the lifeless body. Every second counted with a drowning victim.

"I'm an RN," she said, jaw clenched from nerves and cold.

"Can you handle this?" the surfer asked.

"Yes. But we need a phone to call nine-one-one."

He glanced down the beach where a jogger was headed toward them. The surfer took off after him at a dead run.

Kate examined her patient from head to toe. He was young, really young. That made heart issues less likely. His wetsuit didn't indicate damage to the material or blood, so whatever was wrong with him, it wasn't a shark attack. She felt for a pulse and listened for breaths. He had a pulse. Good.

She adjusted his head to open his airway, listened and felt for breath. Nothing. She readjusted his head. Still nothing. With her lips to his she started mouth-to-mouth resuscitation, her body moving on autopilot through the steps of breathing for him. She needed paramedics if this guy was going to have any chance, and she needed them now.

"Breathe, damn it!" She rechecked his pulse. Weak, but still there. That was something. She put air into his cold, still body. She looked up at the approach of the tall surfer. She could hear enough of his side of the conversation to realize he was communicating with the emergency dispatcher. He must've gotten a phone from that person down the beach.

"He's still unconscious, unresponsive. I have a pulse but no respirations." She breathed again. "How far out is the medic?" Even she could hear the frantic edge to her voice. *Calm down.* She rubbed wet hair out of her eyes and continued to work, the stillness interrupted only by the surfer's terse responses to the nine-one-one dispatcher.

Finally, shrieking sirens broke through the quiet on the beach. She closed her eyes and ushered up thanks. When she opened them, she was gazing directly into the bright blue eyes of the neoprene-clad man kneeling across from her.

"I'd take over but …"

"You can't," she said between breaths. "Unless you're trained?"

"No. The dispatcher told me to let you handle it, until you become unable."

She grimaced. "I'm able. God, they need to hurry!"

Chapter 2

Alec gave the woman kneeling in the sand across from him a long look as she went through the steps of trying to resuscitate the man. Alec stood as men in uniforms exited the emergency vehicles, gathered their equipment, and hustled toward them. Zack paced the beach down by the point, probably confused. Alec whistled for him. His loyal friend's head came up at the sound. Then he bolted toward them. A short mustachioed paramedic and a taller, uniformed medic carrying a rectangular box made their way over.

"Kate?" the man with the mustache asked.

The medic knew the nurse? Not surprising in a town as small as Cielito.

"Whatcha got?" he asked.

Kate gave both men a quick rundown and they exchanged medical jargon with her as they rapidly unloaded equipment and set to work. An expression of acute relief passed over her face as she relinquished the resuscitation efforts to the paramedics. Alec studied her as she sat back on her heels and rubbed a shaking hand over her face. She rose, unsteadily, allowing the medics better access to the patient. Alec frowned. Was she okay? Zack arrived and dropped the ball at his feet. Alec shook his head and walked his dog several feet away from the scene. He did not need him leaping all over the medics, or worse, the victim.

"Zack, sit."

The police officers approached, making their way slowly across the loose sand.

The jogger walked over. Alec handed the man his cell phone. "Thanks."

"No problem."

Silently they waited as the officers walked toward them.

"Lieutenant Stevenson," the taller police officer said, not offering his hand but leaning over to give Zack a pat.

The other uniformed man shook hands with the two men, "Officer Hatch."

"Paul Anderson," the jogger said.

Officer Hatch wrote the name on his pad.

"Alec Sawyer."

Hatch stared at Alec, a confused look on his face. Alec watched the officer work it out, groaning inside as he did. He assumed Hatch was imagining him younger, with longer hair, wearing black, strapped to a guitar. They always did.

"Alec Sawyer? *The* Alec Sawyer?"

Alec nodded. "Yep."

Paul Anderson's eyes narrowed, then widened.

"I'm a huge fan of Bliss," Officer Hatch said.

"Thanks man."

"Seriously, dude. Bliss was freaking awesome." He shook Alec's hand, again.

"Appreciate it. Always nice to meet a fan. So …"

"Any chance you guys might get back together?"

"No." He still got this question and it never ceased to amaze him. Their lead singer, Neal Cooper, died from a drug overdose almost a decade ago and the rest of the members had played in half a dozen bands. Successful bands. With Cooper dead, none of them had any interest in getting the band back together. Sure, they were still friendly—they had been through too much together to harbor any ill will—but they would never be one of those "reunion" bands playing greatest hits from the glory days. The royalties from Reeking Bliss kept them all very comfortable.

Lieutenant Stevenson was younger than his partner and clearly unimpressed. "Can you tell us what happened here this morning?"

Alec ran through the story, as the medics loaded the still figure onto the gurney with the help of two firefighters who'd also joined the scene. The group carried the man's body up to the waiting ambulance, no easy feat in the shifting, slippery sand. Kate made her way to their group, hunched over, arms wrapped around her wet, shivering body.

Alec listened to the officers interview Paul, but his gaze remained on Kate.

"Officers," Alec said. "Do you have a blanket? This poor woman is freezing." She gave him a grateful look. The winds were picking up and despite the protection of his wetsuit, he was chilled. He could only imagine how cold she was in wet running clothes and bare feet.

"Maybe you should get checked out." He eyed her as one of the officers came back from his car with a blue wool blanket.

"No, I'm fine, just c-c-cold."

Sergeant Hatch gave his card to Alec, Kate, and the jogger, asking them to contact him if they remembered anything else that might be relevant. The two officers headed to their patrol car. Kate wrapped the blanket around her, then knelt to give Zack a quick pat.

After a brief farewell, the jogger took off down the beach.

"Kate?" She nodded and he introduced himself, "Alec Sawyer." They shook hands.

She pushed her sopping hair out of her face. He looked down, meeting her eyes and really noticed her for the first time. Her oddly intense, almond-shaped green eyes were luminous and framed by thick black lashes. They were enormous in her pale face. His gaze lingered on her wide mouth, with its perfectly bowed lips. Lips that could give a man seriously inappropriate fantasies, if they weren't blue from the cold. He took in her thick dripping mass of dark red hair, and did a double take when he realized how short she was.

How on earth had she managed to drag that unconscious man to the surface? A hard body she was not. His practiced eye swept over her, the thin damp blanket revealing more than it concealed. Her body was lush. All curves. She was fit, but the overall impression was shapely, not strong. Sexy, but young. He felt of twinge of discomfort. What was he doing checking her out when she was clearly both freezing cold and much too young—besides, she was not his type at all. His type—and he definitely had one—was tall, buxom, and blonde.

"My place is right up the beach. Come with me and dry off, then I'll run you home." He gestured toward the point.

"That's not necessary." She glanced down the beach making it clear to Alec she wasn't comfortable.

"Yeah, it is. You're freezing. Come on." His tone brooked no argument. "Let me grab my board."

There was no sign of the other surfboard, nor of Kate's shoes, on the long cold walk down the beach. Kate threw the ball halfheartedly for Zack a few times, apparently lost in thought.

"So, do you think he'll make it?" Alec finally asked, glancing at her. She looked miserable.

"He has a chance, I guess. His heart was still beating but I have no idea how long he was underwater. I didn't see him go under. It's not good that he didn't regain consciousness or start breathing on his own."

"Right."

She looked over at him.

"I don't even know how long it took me to get to him or how long to get back to the beach, or maybe most importantly, why he went under in the first place…" Her shoulders slumped.

"Do you get used to that, as a nurse? Being in that kind of situation?"

"No way. It's nothing like my job in the hospital. There's death, of course, and in some situations, a lot of stress, so I've been exposed to that. I guess you get a little used to it, but I've never experienced anything like what we just went through." She pulled the blanket tightly around herself. "You're a good man to have in a crisis."

"I was thinking the same of you. I don't know how you dragged him up. He must outweigh you by a hundred pounds." He still couldn't believe it.

She shrugged. "Adrenaline. I was lucky he wore a leash and I'm so glad you were there. There's no way I could have gotten him to shore."

He nodded.

Concern written clearly on her face, she asked, "How do *you* feel?"

"Tired."

She gave a short laugh. "Yeah. Me too. I worked last night."

"You work the night shift?" he asked. "Over at Cielito Community Hospital?"

"Yep. Three times a week."

He made a sympathetic noise. "So why are you out running instead of home sleeping?"

"It's hard to sleep when I first get home. I think I'm still 'up' from my shift, you know?"

"Yeah, I've worked nights before. You need time to chill before you crash. Never thought about going for a run, though."

They trailed the dog as he led them up the sandy, winding, narrow path, flanked by purple flowering ice plants until they reached the house. Alec led the way up to the flagstone patio past the hot tub, fire pit, and outdoor furniture. He propped his surfboard against the stucco house, then gestured for her to follow him. Normally he would've rinsed and peeled off his wetsuit in the outdoor shower, but he couldn't do that with her there. He hosed off their feet and bent to rub the sticky sand first off his toes, then hers. She gasped and pulled her foot away.

"No?" He looked up from his crouch, eyebrows raised.

"I can get it." He sprayed her feet while she rubbed, then he hosed off the dog. Zack shook droplets of water from his thick coat onto both of them. She laughed as the spray showered her. He left Zack to dry off on the patio and ushered her in through the glass door. She followed him through the living room into the kitchen.

"I'll put some coffee on while you hop in the shower." Maybe it would warm her faster. He reached and reflexively touched a rough fingertip to her bloodless cheek. She froze, green eyes widening as she met his gaze. The touch startled him and he withdrew his hand as if burned.

"I'm sorry." What made him do that? "I was thinking you seem awfully pale and wondered if it was the cold or your coloring." He watched, entranced as a flush crept up her neck, into her cheeks.

She ducked her head. "Probably a bit of both. Coffee sounds great."

He led her down the hall to his guest bathroom. Handing her a bath sheet from the linen closet, he backed away.

"I can throw your stuff in the dryer if you toss it out, meantime you can wear the robe hanging on the door."

She thanked him and he padded down the hallway to the kitchen. God. How old was she anyway? Nursing school is two years, maybe four. He rapidly calculated. Even if she'd just gotten out of school she had to be at least twenty. He groaned. Twenty. Even for him that was young.

Moments later footsteps came from the hall. He turned to find a half-naked model standing in his kitchen.

He scowled. "Trinity." This was all he needed this morning. What was she still doing here?

"What the hell Alec? Who is she?" Trinity put her hands on her hips and glared.

He recoiled at her tone. "What?"

"The girl, Alec?" She motioned in the direction of the hall. "Why are you still here?"

He had made it clear in no uncertain terms that she should head back to LA first thing this morning. His teeth ground together.

Their relationship, if that was even the term, had taken an unforeseen turn last night when she arrived, unexpected, uninvited, and definitely unwelcome. Theirs was a no-strings-attached affair of more than a year that had run its course. Sure, it had been mutually satisfying. He took her to parties and introduced her to people who could help her budding acting career, they had a good time in bed—and she had little to no expectations of him. Apparently something had changed on her end. He didn't flatter himself that it was newfound emotional attachment. There was no intimacy in it for either of them.

He sighed. Despite the length of their relationship he hadn't seen this coming. Evidently she had decided to double down on him. The fact that she made the two-hour drive from Los Angeles last night should have clued him in. He never invited girlfriends up here. Never. And today of all days. He was exhausted and had Kate in his guest bathroom.

"I'm not interested in continuing," he gestured between them with his hand, "this."

"That's obvious *now*."

He didn't correct her mistaken impression about the woman showering in the other room. Instead, he waited silent and expressionless as she gathered her things and got dressed.

She stalked out the front door and out of his life. He rubbed a hand across his eyes.

Alec finally had everything: a good career, excellent health, and affluence, a wholly enviable life. His past was an excess of everything: drugs, parties, rock, sex, and money. At the bitter end of his music career, the drugs and alcohol had erased everything good and very nearly erased him. His downfall had been long, spectacular, and public. Sober now for nearly a decade, he was irrevocably changed and mostly for the better.

Why, then, was there this disturbing similarity in the nature of his relationships? He was thirty-eight and sex was still recreation; usually with a succession of much younger model/actresses, and one reality TV starlet. The latter a mistake of nearly catastrophic proportions—thoughts of her brought the term 'stalker' to mind, in a very unfunny way.

Most of the reality stars had their personal dramas exaggerated with careful editing. He suspected hers had been carefully edited to preserve the illusion of sanity. The woman was downright unbalanced. He suppressed a shudder at the memory. It hadn't helped that her show had been wildly popular at the time and her facade of emotional stability rapidly unraveling. When he ended it, she had threatened him and his dog. Zack had to be kenneled for two weeks and the law firm added extra security.

As Alec showered, he struggled to remember the last healthy, intimate relationship he'd had with a woman. He had changed and made coffee by the time Kate met him in the kitchen, swallowed up in one of his white robes.

"I, uh…" She was clearly uncomfortable as she glanced around.

He raised his brows, and then it dawned on him. She was looking for Trinity. She must have heard them.

"Sorry about that. She's gone. I didn't realize she would still be here," he said smoothly, handing her the mug.

"Oh. Okay. Thanks." She accepted the cup and blew on it.

He stared at those lips again, then gave himself a mental shake.

She glanced up. "My clothes shouldn't take too long to dry."

"I'll run you home when they are."

"So, what do you do?" she asked idly, scanning his kitchen.

"I'm in entertainment law, musicians mostly." He studied her reaction. She seemed mildly curious. "I was a musician."

"Here in Cielito?"

"No, the firm I work for is in Los Angeles. I do some work remotely up here and I try to get here several times a week."

"Yeah, I've seen you surfing." She sat on the stool at the kitchen island and hooked an ankle over the bottom rung.

He nodded.

"Why law?"

"I've been asking myself that same question lately."

She watched him with those intense eyes. "Why did you go into it in the first place?"

He thought about his motivations for a moment. It was a fair question. Perhaps he was trying to prevent people from making the same mistakes he had. Maybe it was the search for respectability after the excesses of his past. Most likely, it was because college, then law school had required so much time and energy he didn't have much left over for anything else. Initially, that had been a key to his sobriety.

"I wanted to protect musicians from unscrupulous people. Most of the men and women who have success with their music are young and naive. They get these huge sums of money when they've never had money before, and you wouldn't believe the way they mismanage it. Then there are the parasites who latch on. It's a very ugly business."

She nodded. "I can imagine."

"The problem is, it's tough to convince them to manage their earnings appropriately early on and later, when they get caught up in the dark side of the fame, it's virtually impossible. It's hard to watch." He splayed out his hands and shrugged.

"It's hard to watch people make the same mistakes you made?" she asked, softly.

"So you do recognize my name?" That surprised him. She was a little young to be a fan of Reeking Bliss.

"No. I recognize your intensity. Saving people from themselves is a tough business, isn't it?"

He stared at her, taken aback. This was no twenty-year-old. "Where were you when I needed a career counselor?"

She grinned at him and it stopped the breath in his throat. Her smile was incandescent.

"In high school, probably." She laughed at the expression on his face.

"If it makes you feel any better, I'm guilty of the same. Nurses have a lot of experience trying to save people from their excesses."

"How old are you?" Rudeness be damned.

She grinned. "Twenty-five."

The dryer buzzer sounded and she retreated to put on her running gear. When she returned, he handed her a hooded sweatshirt from the hall closet and insisted she put it on, overriding her protests.

He helped her into his low-slung convertible and she directed him to her residence, a tiny guest house on a large estate. He pulled into her driveway and parked. She turned and thanked him, and was out the door and into her house in a flash. As he sat in the car, he got a whiff of whatever herbal body wash he'd left in the guest shower and something else, something he hadn't smelled in a long time. Innocence.

Chapter 3

"Good God." Ava Bennett's hand froze, a drink midway to her mouth. "Tell me everything." She put the cup down and leaned forward.

Kate watched her friend with a smile.

"Not much to tell." Kate repeated what had happened that morning. They were sitting on Surf Coffee's patio, sipping Chai tea and coffee. Sunlight dappled the patio, filtering through fragrant eucalyptus leaves.

"Was he hot?" Of course that was Ava's next question. Typical Ava.

Kate smiled.

Her mother had said Ava was boy-crazy years ago when they were both thirteen and in middle school. Not much had changed on the inside. Ava was still outgoing, fearless and flirtatious. But on the outside? Eyeing her friend across the table Kate shook her head. Hard to believe the gangly girl with mousy hair, braces, and glasses, grew into the leggy, lean, and gorgeous blue-eyed blonde across from her.

"The guy I tried to resuscitate?" Kate laughed. "I have to say I didn't notice. His lips were cold and blue."

"Gross." Ava frowned. "You know I don't enjoy your nurse humor."

Kate sobered as she considered the guy's chances of recovery. Slim to none would be her guess.

"So…*was* the surfer hot?"

"Yeah."

Ava shot her a suspicious, narrow-eyed look. "Just 'yeah'? I don't think so, girlfriend. You don't get off that easy. Spill!"

Kate grinned. "Yes. He was absurdly hot." Hot was an understatement. He was the most attractive man she had ever seen. Dark hair, strong jaw, brilliant blue eyes, beautiful bone structure, and a nose that wasn't quite straight. Somehow it all added up to an astonishingly sexy male. And his body? Even in a wetsuit he had the body of a god. Had he noticed that she'd been tongue-tied? He was probably used to it.

"All right." Ava made a fist and gave a tiny air pump.

"He's also old."

Ava cocked her head. "How old?"

Kate frowned. "Mid-thirties?"

Ava pursed her lips. "That's not old."

"He's a lawyer—used to be a musician. He must do well, since he has a place right on the beach, near Mar Vista. He took me there to warm up, then he drove me home."

Ava's brows arched, her voice rose an octave. "You went to his *house*? Are you kidding me? That's not safe, girl."

Kate's eyes widened. "For heaven's sake Ava, he helped me rescue a stranger. I think that tells me all I need to know about his character. Besides, as it turns out, we weren't alone."

Ava cocked her head.

"So, I'm standing there, checking for soap, about to close the door when this blonde wearing a skimpy towel comes to the doorway."

"Oh my gosh!"

"I know, right? She was gorgeous, Slavic model hot. So I'm thinking, is this his wife? But before I can even introduce myself, she tells me she's with Alec and I should get lost."

Ava's hand came up to cover her mouth.

"Then she huffs out of there and heads down the hall. I probably should have closed the door at that point but I stood, listening."

"Was it his wife?"

"No. She marched to wherever he was and yelled at him."

Ava's mouth slackened. "Whoa."

"I know. Total player, right? After he told her to leave, I ducked back into the bathroom and started the shower before they could catch me listening."

"Wow."

"He figured out I knew she was there and told me she left."

"Are you going to see him again?"

"What? No. Didn't you hear anything I said after 'he was hot'? Honestly." She ticked the reasons off on her fingers. "He's old. He's a player. Lives in LA. Rich."

"So? You sell yourself short."

"I love you, Ava, but no."

Kate's hand moved to her chest reflexively, then to her neck. Plucking out her shirt, she ducked her chin, leaned back and glanced to her navel. Not there.

Releasing her shirt, she sat forward. She withdrew her hand, heart sinking. *The beach.*

"What is it?" Ava asked.

"My locket. It's gone."

Ava's brows drew together. "Maybe you left it at home?"

Kate shook her head. "I never take it off," she said, almost inaudibly.

"Oh, hon." Ava moved forward to cover Kate's free hand. "Where did you see it last?"

"I'm pretty sure I had it on when I went running …"

"Oh Kate, if you lost it in the water or on the beach …"

Kate pressed her lips together, blinking rapidly.

"Small price to pay." Maybe she would go back and search the beach. She discarded the idea immediately. The tide had come in and gone out. If the locket had fallen off on the beach or in the water, it was gone forever.

"Tell you what. We'll rent one of those metal thingamajigs with the headphones."

Kate gave her a wan smile. "Thanks, but I think we both know it's gone."

"Maybe, but—"

"It's okay." Tears threatened to reveal how she really felt so she changed the subject.

"So, Emma called this morning."

Ava sighed. "What does she need now?"

"She hit me up for money for a ski trip."

"I hope you refused."

"I did—"

"Good."

"—And then I didn't."

"Damn it. After her credit card bill last month? And all the overtime you're working? It's ridiculous."

"I know. I know. I just feel bad for her. If Mom were still alive…"

"She could never have afforded to send Emma to a private college. Are you kidding me? Your mom was a book-keeper."

"We have the money from her life insurance policy—"

"Kate. You're pissing me off. You got loans for nursing school so you didn't have to touch the principal of the life insurance policy. Now you're spending *all* that money on Emma's tuition, working overtime to pay for her room and board and she's into you for money for a ski trip? Where's *your* ski trip?"

Kate shifted uncomfortably in her seat and looked away.

"Seriously? Say no to the ski trip. You have coddled her for—"

"Enough, Ava." Kate scowled. "When she comes home for Christmas, I'm going to lay it all out there for her."

Ava gave her a narrow-eyed stare. "All of it?"

Kate's hand moved automatically to her necklace.

Damn.

"All of it, Kate?" Ava asked, quietly. "Your finances? Even tell her the truth about your dad?

Kate bit her lip. "Yes. It's time she understood about Dad. God, Ava, she won't let up about him. Did I tell you she mentioned trying to find him—"

"Holy shit. That could be dangerous."

Kate rubbed a hand over her face. "She's eighteen now, so it's not *as* dangerous. He couldn't get her college money if he tried. Although, yeah, that's the only reason he'd be interested in us."

Ava's expression was sympathetic as she leaned out, putting a hand on Kate's arm.

"She needs to grow up. And you need to get on with the life of a twenty-something without a dependent. When your mom gave you that locket and asked you to protect Emma, she didn't mean forever. Maybe losing the locket is a sign from your mom?"

Kate studied her hands in her lap, throat thick, willing tears away. Ava would never understand.

"I'm sorry, Kate. About the locket, about everything."

Kate looked down again. "I know. Thanks for listening. How's work going for you?"

Ava laughed. When she wasn't chastising Kate on how to live her life, Ava was Cielito's most in-demand event planner. "The same. I love it though." Her eyes danced as she leaned into Kate. "Last weekend we had a real doozy—second marriage, trophy wife, at the vineyard. Whew. My God, Kate, the dress was so low cut, it was *crazy*. My heart stopped every time she took a deep breath. I thought the minister would have a stroke."

Kate grinned. Ava had the best work stories.

A little while later Kate checked the time on her phone.

"I've got to get home."

"Wait. I got carried away talking about my job. I want to know what's up with that doctor at work?"

Kate felt the heat rise in her neck. She took a quick sip of her stone cold Chai tea to hide her rosy cheeks from Ava.

"He's been really sweet. He found me in the cafeteria eating before my shift Tuesday night and sat with me."

"So what's the story? Is he married?"

"He's separated, papers filed."

"I've seen him in some commercials the hospital keeps running. Quite a catch."

"He is a great catch for the hospital. I still don't know how Cielito Community pulled it off." She shook her head, puzzled. "The guy is a world-class surgeon. Our operating room has never seen so many cardiac patients."

"I don't mean for the hospital, dummy! I mean for you."

Kate glanced at her watch again. "Ava."

"So now you have a lawyer and a doctor interested—"

Kate laughed. "Neither one is interested in me. Get real."

Ava's brow creased. "What is wrong with you? Haven't you looked in the mirror lately?" She stared at Kate. "I swear you had more confidence when we were sixteen. You're a beautiful woman. Believe me, these older, successful guys are in the market for women our age. I see it all the time in my line of work. You'd make a great trophy wife."

Kate grimaced. "I don't want to be a trophy wife." She gave a short, humorless laugh. "I think we might be getting ahead of ourselves here. I've never even had a serious boyfriend."

Uh oh. What was wrong with her? She didn't usually give Ava that kind of opening.

Ava sat forward in her chair, frowning.

Kate leaned back, fixing her friend with a level stare. Here we go again. Ava was gearing up for her recurring lecture series, 'the trouble with Kate'.

Kate held up a hand. "Please don't start. I know what you are going to say and… I agree."

Ava straightened in her chair, brows raised.

Kate didn't want to continue living her life the way she'd lived it for the past few years. Raising Emma and finishing college had been the primary focus of her life for so long. It left little time for anything else. With Emma gone and a stable job with plenty of vacation accrued, she had no excuse. She spent most evenings on her couch curled up with a book. Last weekend she had binged on the entire fourth season of *Dexter*. She hadn't even left the cottage.

Ava was right. Kate had to live. She knew that now. Something shook loose out there in the ocean this morning. In the surf, on that beach, she had experienced the fragility of life firsthand.

It wasn't the first time she's been near death; her mother died young and Kate was inundated with death as a nurse. But old people died. No matter how many advances there were in medicine, it was eventually a losing battle. Young people died in hospitals, too. That was harder to take. She'd seen accidents or injuries take the lives of the young frequently, with devastating consequences for the family and friends.

But nothing, not her mom's early death from cancer, not her work experiences, nothing made her aware of her own mortality until the rescue. She couldn't stop thinking about that guy. She couldn't handle finding out he hadn't made it.

What Ava had been trying to tell her finally made sense. With college behind her, a good career ahead of her and Emma gone, Kate needed to get out of the rut she'd dug herself and do the things she always wanted to do. Travel. Date. Take risks.

She took a deep breath. "What happened with that surfer this morning has made me…think about my life."

Ava reached across the table to grip her hand. Kate squeezed back.

"I'm stuck, Ava. I don't regret waiting for the right person, I just, I just…well, I need to get out more."

Ava clapped her hands, beaming. "Will you let me set you up with someone?"

Kate tried to muster some enthusiasm. "I guess. Although it didn't work out so well last time—"

Ava waved a negligent hand. "I know a couple of great guys."

Kate pressed her lips together to hide a smile. Debatable.

Ava raised her eyebrows. "I see you trying not to smile. You need to open yourself up."

Kate pretended to shudder. "There's nothing wrong with waiting and making absolutely sure it's right."

Ava met and held her gaze.

Kate bit her lip, and looked away.

"You of all people should know there are no absolutes. You just have to dive in there and try. I've never been able to understand your issues around men."

"I wanted to set a good example for Emma—"

"Fat lot of good that did," Ava said.

"Ava!"

"I'm sorry. The fact that you've been saying that since your mom died doesn't make it true. It doesn't even *apply* anymore, now that Emma's not around. I swear that wackadoodle sister—"

"Lay off Emma. I mean it."

"Your sister has healthier relationships with guys than you. I don't know if it's because you lost your mom, or your dad is a nightmare, but whatever it is you need to deal with it."

Kate nodded. "I know. I get it now. That's what I'm trying to tell you."

"Okay then. Let the setups commence."

Kate groaned. "When you put it that way—"

"Why don't you work some overtime so *we* can take a trip?"

Travel. Now that was something she *could* get excited about.

"Yeah. Let's go somewhere." She could swing it with a few more overtime shifts. Or a lot more. Couldn't she?

Ava squealed. "Where? Europe? Australia? Hawaii? Anywhere. And I'm sure my mom would donate some of her frequent flier miles to the cause."

Kate nodded, in perfect accord. "Anywhere. On a budget. But how about somewhere that requires a passport?"

Chapter 4

The incessant vibration of the cell phone woke Kate from a dead sleep and for a moment she was disoriented. The sun shone directly onto her bed. Was it morning or had she been napping? She glanced over at her clock. Eight a.m.? She shot up. After yesterday's excitement she'd slept hard. She grabbed her cell phone from her night-table and stared, blearily, at the display.

Twenty missed calls. Fourteen voice mails. Her eyes narrowed. *What the hell?* She scrolled through the missed calls—local, local, Los Angeles, local, Los Angeles, hospital, Ava. Some came in last night after ten, some calls this morning starting around five am. None from Emma. None from D.C. Whatever was going on, it wasn't about Emma. Kate heaved a sigh of relief.

She scrutinized the numbers again. Three missed calls from the hospital. Nothing new there. They were continually short staffed and trying to get nurses in for over-time. No way was she up for working. Ava had called four times, might as well start there.

The phone vibrated in her hand before she could dial. One of those Los Angeles area codes again.

"Hello?" Her voice was still husky with sleep.

"They're on to us," a rich, deep voice rumbled in her ear.

She pulled the phone away, stared at it, then put it back to her head. "I think you have the wrong number," she said, politely.

He gave a short laugh. "Kate? It's Alec. Did you just wake up?"

She didn't like the way her heart leaped. Was that excitement?

"Oh, Alec. I did. How's it going?" She struggled to keep her tone casual but it came out breathless.

"Have you turned on the TV?"

"No." She tried to stifle a yawn and failed. "What's going on? I have a bunch of missed calls on my phone."

"Good news or bad news first?" he asked, tone serious.

"Good news, please."

"Our surfer is alive and in stable condition. They think he had a seizure."

"Wow." She sat up, riveted. "That's fantastic news! Better than I expected. Incredible."

"Yeah, isn't it? It's a novelty for me, helping save someone's life, but I'm sure you do it all the time."

"Well, no, I mean it happens of course, but not routinely. Most codes…Never mind. What bad news could there possibly be?"

"We've been found out. Someone has been talking and the media is in a lather about it."

What was he talking about?

"The rescue. The media. If they aren't calling you now, they will be."

She drew a sharp breath. "Oh my God."

"Yeah, sorry about this," he said. "I'm…I think I mentioned I'm slightly famous in some circles. Apparently they've tagged me the 'rocker rescuer' and you the 'local nurse heroine' and given the interest in all things celebrity or quasi-celebrity, this thing has gone national."

She sat in stunned silence.

"Kate? Are you with me?"

"Yes," she croaked, hugging her knees to her chest.

"So, ah, I think we have to get in front of this. I know these guys. With or without our cooperation, they'll get their story. The paramedics probably have been interviewed already, the guy who let us use his phone…so they can get what happened from us or …"

"From us?"

"Great."

"Oh, no, that wasn't a statement. That was a question. They want to interview us?"

"Yes. Morning in America—"

"On television? Yikes." Her heart rate tripled.

He sighed. "This won't go away. Trust me, I know from experience. If we get out in front of this train we can direct it, but there is no derailing it. This is the stuff that those weekly entertainment magazine folks live for. Hell, if you present right, you might even get a book deal."

Television? A book deal? Was he nuts?

"Can you stop talking?"

He laughed.

"I have a couple of days off, then I have work…"

"Oh, your work is totally on board with this. These kinds of things can put a little community hospital on the map. Some of the information on you is probably coming from them. I didn't have any trouble getting your number from the hospital, once I explained who I was."

She licked her lips, mouth dry. "Geez."

"Sorry Kate. It's my fault." His tone softened. "If I hadn't been there, the news might have picked up on this local nurse saves surfer thing, likely it would have stayed regional. But with me in the picture it exploded. My agent and firm are fielding calls from most of the major media organizations and all the morning programs in New York. If it helps, there might be some money in this, other than travel, per diem and stuff—"

"What? I don't want money for…what we did."

"Me neither. But I don't think either of us can afford to sit back and let the media have their way with us. If you're up for it, my firm would like us to take the first non-stop to New York for the morning programs tomorrow. So we can put the story out there on our terms."

"Yeah. Um, can I say no? I don't want to do….any of that. Thank you though. I mean, you're really kind and I'm sure…"

"You can say no. I don't want to pressure you, but I think it's only fair if I warn you about what could happen if we don't do this."

He sighed again. "Seriously, I get it. Believe me, I totally get why you don't want to do this. I don't want to either. The last thing I want is the media back in my life. We didn't have much time to talk yesterday, but I got sober and left the music industry nearly a decade ago. I'm sober now, but I didn't leave my old life on a high note. While I was using I did every cliché rock star thing—wrecking cars, fights, jail. I trashed houses and hotel rooms, did court mandated stints in rehab, was too drunk to perform at shows."

"Which band?"

"Reeking Bliss."

"Bliss? I listened to them in middle school," she said. "That's your band?"

"Was, yes. I was the guitarist." He went on doggedly, "That was my life. Not anymore. Now I'm mostly an upstanding member of society, but of course they're still dredging up the bad behavior."

She could hear bitterness in his voice. "I'm really sorry."

"Yeah, well. That's my past. I have to own it, even if I'm not that guy anymore. If you don't talk to the press, they will interview anyone and everyone about you. It can be nasty. Ex-boyfriends with not-so-funny anecdotes, co-workers, family ..."

"No!"

"I'm sorry Kate, but that is exactly what they'll do. They might do it anyway. They'll get the good stuff, but they love dirt too... what kind of dirt are we talking about?"

"Well, I don't want my sister hounded for one thing," she admitted. "She's a freshman in college in D.C."

"Okay, anything else? You are talking to the king of dirt here, baby. I think there are sex tapes of me out there somewhere."

"Yikes." She was startled into a laugh. "I'm sorry. I shouldn't laugh. Nothing that bad. Oh. I'm sorry!" she apologized and tried again, "I didn't mean bad, for you, you're a guy."

"There is no such thing as a good sex tape, Kate. I think if it's any good, they call it porn."

She laughed again.

"So that's what will happen? They'll talk to all those people?"

"Guaranteed. Damage control, spin, image and public relations, are all a part of my job, so I know how this will go down."

She blew out a breath.

"Can you meet me at the airport?"

"I guess." Her heart raced. *Relax.*

"I'll come get you," he said.

"That's not necessary,"

"You're on my way. Be there in an hour." He disconnected the phone before she could say another word.

A call to Ava would burn up the time she needed to pack, so she texted her best friend and promised to call as soon as she could. She packed, desperately trying to ignore the cell phone buzzing like an angry insect every few minutes. It was hard to put two thoughts together.

Maybe Emma could meet her in New York? It wasn't that far from D.C., was it?

Less than an hour later, a black town car pulled into the driveway. She grabbed her purse and her rolling bag, took a deep breath, and stepped through the threshold, locking the door behind her.

Chapter 5

Clearly fate was in full agreement with her decision to take more risks with her life. Here she was, on a plane, in first-class, on her way to do television talk shows in New York. Sitting next to an insanely hot guy. Not that he'd be interested in her, cheek stroking aside. She watched him out of the corner of her eye.

He was dressed casually for the flight in a close-fitting long-sleeved navy henley that did amazing things for both his powerful chest and well-defined arms. Who was she kidding? His chest and arms did amazing things for the shirt. Worn jeans, faded nearly white in some areas, encased slim hips and muscular thighs. She had gaped at his denim clad rear earlier at the airport. The man looked shockingly good in jeans; then again, he looked good in a wetsuit, which she hadn't thought possible.

Kate's phone rang as she buckled into the window seat next to Alec. She had been just about to turn it off, but checked the display.

Emma.

"Emma? I only have a minute. The plane is going to take off."

"I'm so excited. I'll take the train up and meet you tonight."

"Cool. I'll text you the hotel info, okay?"

"I just got out of class and got your message. I can't believe you're going to be on national television. You rock! My friends are all going to be watching you tomorrow."

Kate froze. The air rushed out of her lungs.

Oh no!

National television.

"Kate?"

"I…I have to go."

"Okay, call me when you land. I'm so excited!"

Kate pressed the red end button on the phone with nerveless fingers and slid it into her purse. A wave of panic swept through her. The seat in front of her swam and she closed her eyes, taking deep breaths.

Matt Gibson. What had she been thinking? Clearly she hadn't. She couldn't risk being on television. What if her dad saw her? No. She couldn't do it.

She snuck a glance at Alec. He was frowning at his phone, mouth pulled tight. He turned his phone off with a sigh and leaned forward to shove it into his pocket. The flight attendant notified passengers that departure of the aircraft was imminent.

She'd just have to plead…terror?

But they're paying for this flight, the hotel room.

She pressed her lips together. They couldn't *make* her go on. Surely people had chickened out before?

Alec met Kate's alarmed gaze.

"Everything all right?" he asked with a warm smile.

Kate grimaced. "Yep."

Stress turned to fear and the hole in the pit of her stomach grew as the plane picked up speed down the runway. It left the ground, her stomach lurched and she turned away from the window, closing her eyes. She felt his large, warm calloused palm take hers. She didn't dare open her eyes, focusing all her energy on keeping the plane aloft.

It seemed like forever before the pitch leveled out. Taking a deep breath, she opened her eyes. Alec's blue gaze registered sympathy and concern. She tugged her hand but his grip tightened. Butterflies started up in her stomach again, but for a completely different reason.

"First time on a plane?" he asked.

"Third." The take-off was the most disturbing part.

His eyes widened.

"Excitement and nerves," she said. "I'm not really scared." She gave another small tug and he released her hand, smiling.

"So where did you go, last time you flew?"

"I took my sister, Emma, to see at colleges on the East Coast about a year and a half ago."

"Where did she end up going?"

"She fell in love with Washington, D.C. as much as the college. We looked at schools in Virginia and Maryland too." Kate shook her head. "But she's a city girl. I don't imagine she'll come back to Cielito after college. She'll end up in New York or stay in D.C."

"You say that like it's a bad thing."

"She's my only family and I want to be close to her." Kate sighed. "But I don't want to leave California. I love Cielito."

"Cielito is amazing. Is Emma your only family?"

Kate pushed her hair out of her eyes. "Yeah. My parents divorced when I was seven, just after my mom got pregnant with Emma. My mom died of cancer when I was eighteen."

"I'm so sorry."

"Thanks. It was a long time ago, but we were close. My mom was amazing."

"Do you talk to your dad at all?"

She met his gaze. "We don't have any contact with my father. He's not a very nice person," she said.

"Oh, then who raised Emma?"

Her chin lifted. "I did."

He gave a low whistle. "That had to be really hard. How did you make ends meet?"

"My mom had a modest life insurance policy. And we had friends to help. I went to college on a scholarship. The bulk of what's left goes to Emma's tuition." It hadn't been easy but they'd managed.

He reached and squeezed her hand. The slight touch tingled through her.

"Damn." His voice was soft.

"What?"

"Well, if I think you're remarkable, I shudder to think how the media will portray you." That smile, those eyes, they did funny things to her pulse rate.

She hadn't a clue what to say to that, but she felt her cheeks heat. "Thanks. I think. It wasn't a hardship. I was old enough to take care of her."

"So why nursing?"

"Why not?"

"Well, after what you went through, watching your mom die, I would think you would steer clear of healthcare."

"Mostly practical reasons."

"How so?"

"The pay is decent, the hours flexible—I could work longer shifts, be home more, and I was pretty much guaranteed a job in town. Those were the most important considerations then."

"Because of Emma?"

"Yeah."

"Do you regret it? Following the practical path?"

"Do *you* regret following the practical path?"

"We're not talking about me." His smile erased the sting from his words and made her breath hitch.

She shrugged. "I did what I had to do. I haven't spent a lot of time contemplating other options. I like nursing, I don't love it. Will I do something else someday? Who knows?"

She pulled the celebrity magazine she'd purchased in the airport out of the seat pocket in front of her.

Alec nodded to it. "They called, by the way. Asked to interview us."

"No way."

"They do a human interest story each week. You can either do a phone interview or wait two days until we are back on the west coast and they'll send someone up from LA."

She shook her head. "I'll pass." She rubbed a hand over her face. This whole thing was so complicated. All this media attention. She could only hope her father didn't find out. Could she ask Alec to keep her name out of it? She'd deal with backing out once they landed.

"You seem very used to this whole thing. So, what does an entertainment lawyer do anyway?"

"A little of this, a little of that."

She raised her brows.

"I don't get to spend as much time doing what I'd like to, which is negotiating contracts, setting up charitable foundations, and advising on asset management because…" He rubbed a hand over his chin.

"Because?"

He gave her a sardonic look. "I spend most of my time dealing with the fall-out from my clients' bad behavior and poor choices."

"Ah."

"Yeah. Once the money flows, the crazy multiplies, especially in rock."

"I'll bet. I've seen a few episodes of *Behind the Music*."

He grinned. "Then you know exactly what my job is like."

"I did a quick search on you online."

"I hope you didn't see the sex tape." He winked.

She felt the heat start up her neck and wash over her face. He stared at her with a fascinated air that made her blush more and turn away.

"You do that a lot." He gestured to her face, with that sexy half-grin.

"You'll be happy to know I didn't encounter the video. Even if I had, I wouldn't watch it. I'd never be able to look you in the eye again."

"So now you know I used to be perpetually screwed up."

"I only had time to read the Wikipedia entry on you and Reeking Bliss. No music anymore?"

He touched his chin, brow wrinkled. "No."

"Oh."

"I got out for a good reason."

"I can understand that. People, places, things. Right? But that was ten years ago."

"Yeah." His body was rigid. Clearly, he didn't want to discuss it.

"Well, you seem to have conquered your demons."

He gave her a sharp look. "You're a nurse. You know how it goes with that."

"I do. You can never get too comfortable. Do you think you'll get back into music?"

"No, but who knows?" He quoted her words back at her with a smile.

Interesting. He didn't care for his current job but he wasn't sure enough of his sobriety to risk returning to music.

She opened her magazine and read until the words blurred. Pulling off her jacket, she stuffed it up against the window. The vibration of the plane, the drone of the engine, were the last things she noticed before nodding off to sleep.

The intercom crackled. "We're beginning our approach to Kennedy, folks."

She blinked and stretched, then pulled on her jacket.

Alec glanced over at her. "I envy your ability to fall asleep."

She nodded. "You learn quickly when you work nights to take the sleep when you can get it."

He handed her a bottle of water.

"Thanks."

Kate and Alec arrived, disembarked and made their way through the terminal.

She glanced around. This airport was enormous.

Biting her lip, Kate chanced a look at Alec, pulling his carry-on beside her.

"Uh, Alec?"

"Yep."

"How are we getting to the hotel? Is there a van or—"

"Nah. The show is taking care of transportation. There should be a driver holding up a sign with our names near baggage claim."

Oh good.

Should she tell him now? No. At the hotel. She'd tell him at the hotel. But then he'd try to talk her into it. Tomorrow. First thing.

Kate gripped the rail on the escalator. Alec's tall form was slightly ahead of her and easy to track in the crowd. She spotted a thickset man in a black suit with a sign near the bottom of the escalator that read: "Alec Sawyer".

Alec approached the man, shook his hand and Kate wheeled her bag up to them.

"Ready?" the man in the black suit asked, gesturing to the exit.

Kate smiled and nodded, sliding up next to Alec. They had almost reached the automatic doors when a voice called out, "Alec Sawyer?" Alec's body brushed against hers as they walked and she felt his body tense. He turned, and with a polite smile, faced the man who hailed him.

Kate glanced from Alec to the well-groomed businessman, shuffling his feet.

She stayed close to Alec. His body was still stiff, smile polite, distant.

"Yes?"

"*The* Alec Sawyer? The guitarist for Reeking Bliss?"

He took two steps toward Alec, radiating excitement. Alec moved forward and away from the doors.

"Yes."

They shook hands, as the man, "a big fan," introduced himself.

Alec looked over his shoulder at Kate. "Will you excuse me a minute?"

"Sure."

Did he know all these people?

Two more men moved closer to Alec. Kate watched wide-eyed as more and more people gathered to get pictures and shake Alec's hand.

The people and their requests kept coming. Alec was getting swallowed up in the little crowd. She moved forward to get a better look. His expression was friendly, but not open the way it was with her. People asked him about Bliss.

"Will you guys get back together?"

"Are you here in New York to perform?"

He shook his head, smiling. People took surreptitious pictures of him with their phones. Other people around her murmured, wondering who he was.

"Is he an actor?"

"Who is that?"

A group of girls younger than Emma giggled. "God. He's hot."

Kate grinned. She had to agree.

Two statuesque brunettes whispered excitedly to one another before approaching him. They asked a bystander to get a photo of them posing with Alec. Each put an arm around him. One kissed his cheek and the other chatted him up. The taller brunette pushed a piece of paper into Alec's hand.

Smiling slyly, he tucked it into his jeans pocket.

Kate's mouth dropped open. *Good Lord!* Was it that easy for him? Yikes.

He allowed a few more pictures and autographs before he backed away, she heard him making excuses.

He rejoined her and the driver and the three of them made their way to the town car.

"Does that happen often?" she asked.

Alec wasn't exactly besieged, but she was surprised people recognized him.

"Not often, no." He held the car door for her, as the driver loaded their bags into the trunk. She scooted across the leather seat.

"Most people don't remember what I look like since I've been out of the public eye for a number of years. Occasionally, a real die-hard Bliss fan will want something signed. Hold up a sign with my name at a New York airport?" He smiled, glancing meaningfully at the driver, who was pulling out into traffic. "Yeah, some Bliss fans come out of the woodwork. That's okay. I only mind when they show up at my house."

Kate's hand went to her throat. "Oh, my God."

"I had to install security systems in my homes in Los Angeles and Cielito."

"Geez." She sat back and peeked up at him.

"It was worse back in the day. Bliss had a real cult following, but Cooper got the brunt of the crazies."

He hadn't even played for ten years. When he told her on the phone that his past followed him around she hadn't understood what that meant. Not until now. Something a lot like sympathy bloomed inside her.

Because of rush hour traffic, it took ages to get from the airport to the hotel the show had booked for them, but Kate didn't mind. She rolled down the window a bit and got a good view of the skyline. Alec worked, tapping out texts and emails on his phone, but she caught his amused glance.

She smiled widely. "Am I gawking?"

"It's cute. It's fun to be with someone who's experiencing New York for the first time. I don't even remember my first visit."

"No? It's incredible. The smell—"

He laughed. "The smell?"

"It smells different here, the trees—"

"All I smell is exhaust."

There were dropped off in front of one of the most expensive, exclusive hotels in the city off Central Park. Horse drawn carriages waited across the street. The lobby was elegant and understated with wood paneling, recessed lighting, and old style lamps. Alec and Kate took the elevator up to their floor. He followed, making sure her key card worked. He pushed her door open and she walked past.

"Wow."

The room was opulent and elegantly understated, with stunning views of the skyline. She felt a twinge of guilt and bit her lip. The television program was paying for all this and she wasn't even going to go on.

Alec glanced around. "Nice. Let's switch rooms," he offered. "They put me in a suite and you'll need the extra room with your sister staying. It's right down the hall.

"Oh, no. I can't let you do that. If yours is bigger—"

"Sure you can." He handed her his key card, and slid hers from her fingers. "You'll spend more time looking out the window than I will. Guaranteed." He left his bag in the room and she followed him down the hall to the opposite side of the building. He used his key card to open the door and indicated she should enter. His suite was much larger, with views of Central Park and a telescope for bird or people watching.

"Thanks, Alec." The guilt surged up and she knocked it down. It couldn't be helped. Kate checked her watch. "Emma's train arrives in half an hour. She should be here soon."

"We have to be at the studio around six a.m. tomorrow morning." He headed for the door. "Meet in the lobby at five-thirty?"

"Great."

With a jaunty wave, he pulled open the door and disappeared though the doorway. The heavy door closed soundlessly behind him.

Chapter 6

"Emma." Kate rapped on the bathroom door. "We need to go. We're going to be late."

They *were* late. Alec was probably cooling his heels in the lobby. Damn it. Of all times for Emma to be running behind.

Emma opened the door grumbling. "Keep your shirt on. Geez."

Kate checked her phone for the third time in five minutes. Should she tell Alec now? She didn't want to have to go to the studio.

"We're officially late." Kate grabbed the key card and her bag. "You can meet us down there or take a cab."

She needed to get to the lobby and tell him she couldn't do it. That way he could go without them. Now they had made him late.

"No, no. I'm ready," Emma replied, scuttling around the room, collecting her things from where they were strewn on the floor and over various items of furniture.

Kate twisted her hands together in the elevator and took a deep breath. Would he be angry? She hoped not. He'd been so nice, giving up his room and everything.

Alec was standing in the lobby near the concierge when Kate and Emma arrived.

"Ready, ladies?" Alec asked with a cheerful smile.

"Uh…actually, Alec…I," Kate said.

Alec put a hand behind her back and steered her toward the doors, Emma trailing behind. "Can you tell me in the car?"

Kate bit her lip. What should she say? This was *hard*. He was so nice. And Emma was going to be really disappointed.

Tough.

Kate sat next to Emma on the wide leather seat, across from the glass partition separating the driver.

She glanced at Emma.

Emma caught her eye, nodded to Alec and mouthed "hot."

Kate widened her eyes, shaking her head. She adjusted her neckline, her fingers searching for, but not finding the locket.

Emma's hazel eyes narrowed. "Where's Mom's locket?"

Alec looked up from his phone, eyebrows raised.

Kate bit her lip. "I lost it."

"You *lost* it? After all this time? Where?"

"On the beach." Kate frowned at her sister with a small shake of her head.

"Oh, Kate!"

"You lost your mom's locket on the beach that day?" Alec asked, giving her a direct look.

Kate waved a hand airily. "It's okay. It wasn't valuable or anything."

"It was invaluable," Emma insisted. "You haven't taken it off since Mom died, not even to *shower.*"

Kate blew out a breath with exasperation. "Yes. It sucks. It really sucks, but it's *gone.*"

"Did you try—" Emma said.

Her throat thickened and she stared up at the roof. "Emma. Please. Not now."

Emma pressed her lip together mutinously, but remained silent.

The limo pulled up to the studio.

"Wait. I…I can't." Kate said.

Alec and Emma stared at her.

"Can't what?" Emma said.

Kate took a deep breath. "I can't do this."

The driver opened the door. Kate scooted over and closed it.

Alec put a hand out to her.

"It's normal to be scared. You can do it, trust me. You'll be nervous but you'll loosen up." He shot her a crooked grin.

Kate shook her head. Once. Hard. She met Alec's gaze evenly. "No."

Emma started to protest. "But, Kate—"

"I mean it. I'm not going on the show. I'm sorry." Kate's eyes filled with tears and she covered her face with her hands.

Raising her head, she whispered, "Please."

Alec sighed. "All right. I'll explain. You sit with Emma in the studio audience. Will that work?"

Kate let out the breath she hadn't realized she'd been holding. "Yes."

Emma was staring at her wide-eyed. "Kate, what the hell?"

Kate ignored her. Alec opened the door and they filed out. Once inside the building their group was hustled into elevator and up to the studio.

An assistant took Emma to her seat in the front row. Kate followed and took the seat next to her. The woman looked down at her clipboard and frowned.

"I'm only supposed to seat the sister," she said. "Who are you?"

"I'm the other sister."

She cocked her head. "The one who made the rescue?"

"Yeah. I've decided not to go on."

The woman raised her eyebrows and her lips twisted. "I'll have to get the okay on that. You can sit there in the meantime."

She strode away.

"I can't believe you, "Emma hissed. "What's wrong? Why don't you want to go on?"

Kate glanced at her, settling herself onto the padded seat. "I don't want to be on television."

Emma frowned. "Then why did you come?" Her eyes widened. "Oh. Free trip to New York. Brilliant."

Heat rose in Kate's cheeks. "No, I...I thought I could. But I can't."

Emma shrugged. "Whatever. After this we can spend the day together."

Kate and Emma sat through endless news updates. Finally they showed clips of the town of Cielito and surfers riding waves.

Alec walked out, glanced at Kate in the audience and gave her a little wave. He shook hands with Bethany Lucas and Jim Robinson, the co-hosts, before taking a seat on the couch. Alec's dark gray suit fit him perfectly, only his longish hair kept him from looking outrageously conservative.

Kate perched on the edge of her chair.

The hostess frowned. "We thought there would be two guests this morning…" She glanced over her shoulder at the producer shaking his head.

"Yeah, well, you'll have to make do with me this morning. She's shy."

Bethany Lucas laughed. "She is?"

Jim Robinson peered out into the bright lights. "Is she *here*?" He pressed a hand to his ear and announced, "They tell me she's here. Redhead in the front row."

Kate stiffened in the seat, afraid to draw a breath.

Alec lost his smile.

"Aww. Tell her to come on up. We'll be gentle," Bethany said.

A man in a faux western shirt with very short hair covered by headphones, and an electronic tablet in one hand, tried to draw Kate out of her chair.

Kate struggled. The audience laughed.

Jim Robinson stood up, beckoning.

"There she is!" Bethany Lucas announced gaily.

Cameras swung in their direction. Kate stilled mid-struggle and tried to block Emma from the cameras. There were several directed at them and she didn't know which was on. Rather than get into a wrestling match with the determined chic gentleman with the vise-like grip, Kate allowed herself to be pulled toward the stairs and onto the stage.

There was applause and laughter from the audience. Kate felt her cheeks warm. A staff member clipped a microphone on her dress and gave her a push in the direction of the set.

Bethany took her hand and winked at her. Alec stood, and led her shaking body to the couch next to him.

"So Alec, can you tell us what happened?" Bethany asked.

Alec recounted the events of that morning. Kate watched his lips as he spoke, mesmerized by that beautiful mobile mouth. He laughed at something the host said, revealing teeth slightly uneven on the bottom row. She could've watched him talk forever, his square jaw moving, his sensual lips opening as he said… *Wait, what's he saying?*

She sat forward, eyes wide with alarm. *Oh my God*. Here she was on live national television mooning over Alec Sawyer and paying no attention whatsoever to what he was saying. How long had she been staring at him?

She tuned in to hear an absurdly modest re-telling of his role in the rescue. He credited Kate with noticing the missing surfer, recovering him, leading the charge to the beach and the rescue breathing.

"Did you think it could've been a shark attack?" The hostess was clearly enamored with Alec. If she moved any closer she'd be sitting on him.

Alec shook his head. "No. Shark attacks on surfers are rare. When it happens, it's usually because the outline of the board below the water looks like a seal. We're more of a threat to them than they are to us. Lots of surfers have seen sharks—"

"Have you?" Bethany asked, leaning forward, titillated.

Alec shrugged. "Sure. I've been surfing in California for fifteen years. They don't bother me and I don't bother them."

She gave a little shudder. "You're very brave." Bethany actually batted her eyes at him. Kate fought with a grin and lost.

Alec had a polite smile, what she had come to think of as his airport smile, firmly in place. How disturbing that she was able to differentiate between his smiles after two days. She was as smitten as this television hostess.

Jim, the male co-host, turned to Kate with his thousand megawatt smile. He led her gently, as though he'd seen a lot of nervous people on this couch. He started with a few questions about her job and Cielito, before asking for details about the rescue. Eager to set the record straight, Kate forgot to be nervous and launched into her take on the events of that morning.

"I couldn't have gotten the man, Doug, out of the water without Alec. And without Alec calling nine-one-one, Doug would've had no chance, so I have to take issue with Alec's version of things." She shook her head at him.

The reporter nodded, his silence encouraging Kate to continue.

"The Cielito paramedics, firefighters, and police who responded did a great job. And of course, I have to mention the wonderful team at Cielito Community Hospital who are still caring for him."

"Yes, but it was a very brave thing you did. Your parents must be very proud of you," Bethany said.

Kate swallowed, caught off-guard. To her horror, her throat thickened. Blinking rapidly to hold back tears, she turned instinctively to Alec. He leaned toward Kate, and captured her hand.

"Kate's father wasn't around. When her mother died, cancer, right Kate?"

She nodded.

"Kate raised her younger sister," he said.

There was a collective gasp from the audience.

She looked out into the sea of faces, spotted Emma and the sisters exchanged tearful smiles.

"She's an amazing woman. I know her sister is proud of her." He squeezed her hand and she returned the squeeze, indebted to him. The last few moments of the interview, Jim turned a glittering smile on Alec.

"You two seem very comfortable. Rescue leads to romance?" His gaze lingered on their still joined hands, a knowing smile on his thin lips.

Kate's body stiffened.

What the heck? They met the day before yesterday!

"No." She blurted, tugging her hand from Alec's. She felt more than saw Alec brace himself. She racked her brain. She couldn't embarrass him after he covered for her mini-break down on national television.

"He's a lawyer." Tense with nerves, it came out a lot more horrified than she intended.

The audience laughed and Alec's eyes lit with merriment. He put his hand to his chest as if she had wounded him deeply and there was more laughter from both the co-hosts and the audience.

"There you have it folks," Bethany said. "The transformation from bad-boy to model citizen is complete. We want to thank Alec and Kate for acting so heroically and making this world a better place. I know there's a surfer out in California who owes his life to the two of you."

The hostess turned away to face the audience. "Thanks for being with us this morning." They went to commercial. Kate closed her eyes and prayed her father wasn't watching.

Chapter 7

Kate and Emma took the limo back to the hotel. Alec had several more talk shows and interviews. Exhausted, Kate wanted nothing more than to go upstairs and curl up in that big hotel bed until her flight out tomorrow. She looked longingly at the elevator bank.

"I need coffee, Em, if I'm going to keep up with you today."

"I can't believe we get to spend the day together in New York City," Emma squealed. "If only I didn't have an exam tomorrow. I miss you, Kate."

"Me too, Em. More than you know. What should we do?"

"Shop," Emma said.

Kate tensed and a groan escaped her.

Emma narrowed her eyes.

"How about some tourist stuff instead, like the Empire State Building or Times Square?"

Emma's lips stretched into a thin line. "No. And no museums. D.C. is full of museums. Please, Kate, the shopping in New York is to die for."

Kate stifled a sigh. "We can't spend all day shopping. Why don't we go to Central Park or Times Square first?" And hopefully, run out of time for shopping.

Emma agreed with bad grace. "Fine."

"It's a compromise." She smiled at Emma who wouldn't meet her gaze.

Why did it have to be so difficult? Why couldn't Emma understand that her college costs precluded things like a shopping spree in New York? Kate was stretched pretty thin these days but it was never any use pleading poverty with her sister. Emma would just bring up the insurance money. What was left of the insurance money would barely cover her tuition at the private college she attended, never mind room, board, and books.

"Just…please, Kate, I'll go along to your tourist spots if you promise we can hit Bergdorf's before my train."

Kate gave a short nod. "But how much—"

Emma sigh was long and loud. "I don't know how much I'll need Kate. I haven't been there."

Kate twisted her hands together. Emma had zero ability to budget and claimed her class schedule was too rigorous to get a part-time job. They would fight and end the day on a bad note, with Kate falling into her nay saying ways. Something of her conflict must have registered on her face, because Emma examined her closely.

"Don't worry, I won't break the bank," she said, softly.

Emma gave her a one-armed hug and just like that, Kate's frustration vanished. It was impossible to stay mad at her sister.

As they wandered the city, Emma chatted about friends and school and Kate studied her. She'd never known anyone like Emma—incredibly naive, good-natured, and volatile. So volatile. Emma felt things viscerally, but her ease bouncing back from major and minor setbacks in life was awe-inspiring. Parenting Emma through the traumatic high school years had been agonizing. Granted, Kate had always been more emotionally stable than Emma. But lately she wondered if it was easy to be stable when you didn't take risks. Was she cautious to a fault, self-protective and responsible because she'd had to be or because that was her nature? Whichever. She promised herself and Ava that she would step out of her comfort zone.

Kate considered her sister. Though they shared the shape of their mother's eyes and her mouth, Emma had fine straight, strawberry-blonde hair and hazel eyes. She was taller than Kate, but not by much.

A few hours later, they sat outside a bakery, eating pastries and people watching. Emma was talking and Kate realized she'd tuned her sister out.

"I'm sorry, Em. What were you saying?"

"I'm going to try to find him. Just thought you should know."

Kate stared, breath frozen in her lungs.

"Why do you always react like this when I bring up Dad?" Emma frowned. "It's natural to be curious. My friends at school wonder why I've never even met him."

"Emma. We weren't *adopted*. We've lived in the same town our whole lives. If he wanted to know us, he could have." A tiny lie, as lies went.

"I want to meet him," she insisted, stubbornly. "The holidays will be here in a couple of weeks. Maybe he'd want to spend them with us."

Kate couldn't keep the horror from her expression. "I don't think he's a good guy."

"You always say that. What does that even mean?"

"It means I think he's a creep." Kate picked her pastry apart, schooling her features into neutrality.

"Do you remember him?"

"Well, no, not really." Kate could feel her sister's eyes boring holes in her and refused to meet them, keeping her expression carefully blank and her eyes on her plate.

"Did Mom tell you he was a creep?" Emma pressed.

Kate took a sip of her tea to wet her suddenly dry mouth. "No. The Morgans did. Mom didn't mention him much."

Be vague.

Emma cocked her head. "Don't quote Diana and Roy Morgan to me. You've always put too much stock in what they say."

"How can you say that, Emma? The Morgans were Mom's best friends. They helped with *everything* after she died."

Emma shrugged. "Don't you think it's weird he hasn't tried to contact us? I mean, he's our father. And if it was about child support, now that I'm eighteen he doesn't have to worry about that."

"Honestly, I don't think contacting him is a good idea. Diana says—"

"Well, I want to meet him and decide for myself." She crossed her arms over her chest. "And I'm tired of hearing about what Diana says. It's not her family."

Kate closed her eyes behind the sunglasses. "I don't want you to contact him. I'm serious, Emma."

"I don't care," she said, equally firm, "I'm going to try to find him."

Heart racing, desperate, Kate tried the truth. "Em, he's a really bad person."

"How do you know?" Emma narrowed her eyes. "Have you had contact with him?"

"No," she said.

"Well. It's my decision." She gave Kate a nod, then smiled. "Let's not fight about it, 'kay?"

Kate tossed enough money on the table to cover their drinks and desserts then stood, looking at her sister. Emma didn't always follow through on things. Maybe school would keep her busy enough that she wouldn't pursue it. Maybe their father would be hard for her to find.

"So, what kind of things are you going to need for the ski trip?" Kate asked.

Emma looked up, brows creased. "What ski trip?"

Kate's eyes widened. "The ski trip you need five hundred dollars for?"

Emma turned away, "Oh. Oh, yeah." She gave a strangled laugh "Everything's included."

Kate peered at her, frowning. "Everything? What about a ski jacket? All you have is your coat and—"

"Don't worry about it okay? I can borrow what I need. C'mon. Onward." Emma pulled away and led them to the street to flag a cab. Kate watched her retreating back, puzzled.

A cab drove up. Emma opened the door, scooting into the rear seat.

"Bergdorf's, please." Kate said, climbing in. They settled into the pleather seat.

Emma's cell phone rang and she squealed. "Kate, mind if I get this? That's Angie's ringtone."

Kate waved her hand and stared out the window, lost in thought.

Before she died, their mother, Marilyn Gibson, insisted Kate wasn't to contact their father, Matt. She refused to say why and each time Kate brought it up her mom became more and more agitated until finally Kate stopped mentioning him. After her mother's death, in search of answers, Kate brought up the issue of their father with her mom's best friend Diana Morgan. Diana had arranged a meeting with the lawyer, Aldrich, who handled the will. She clearly remembered sitting in the legal office with Aldrich and Diana.

"What about our dad?" Kate said. "Shouldn't he get custody of Emma instead of me?"

"Over my dead body," Diana said.

"I think, Ms. Gibson, if you review these documents, you'll see why we want you to have custody," the attorney said, quietly.

Both people in the room looked at her with varying degrees of pity.

Kate eyed the thick file in his hands. "Marilyn Gibson" was written in pen on the front and at the tab. Aldrich handed it to Kate and she opened the folder, flipping through the papers and pausing to skim each one.

Legal documents, police reports, court filings, Polaroids… Shock fled and horror took its place. She hunched over, fingers trembling, stomach leaden. This was what her mother couldn't tell her about her father? This was why he was never mentioned?

Shaking her head, Kate went through the papers again, calculating dates. She paused and held a hand to her increasingly sick stomach, then moved it to cover her mouth. Kate lurched out of the chair, dumped the papers from her lap and fell to her knees.

Diana grabbed the trashcan from behind the desk and put it in front of her.

When there was nothing left in her stomach, Kate sat weakly and stared at the floor.

"I'm so sorry, honey," Diana whispered. "There is no easy way to tell you these things and your mom couldn't."

*

"Kate? Kate?" Emma gave her a strange look. "Sheesh. You were totally zoned out." The cab had stopped. Kate fixed a smile firmly to her mouth before paying the cabbie. When Emma turned eighteen Kate had finally stopped looking over her shoulder. There was no way she would let Emma bring that man into their lives now. No way.

Chapter 8

The hotel room phone rang, jolting Kate out of her reverie. How long had she been in the bathtub anyway? She had needed to soak the city grime off after a day of running around Manhattan with Emma. Exhausted and hungry, she eyed the corner of the bathroom that housed the toilet and a phone. This place was outrageous. Why was there a phone next to the toilet anyway? Gross. She wrapped herself in the luxurious white bath sheet and picked up the receiver with a wet hand.

"Kate?" a familiar male voice asked.

Her heart leapt in her chest, then accelerated. She heard his voice, her body responded. Not good. "Hey, Alec."

"Did I wake you?"

"No, I was taking a bath."

There was a long silence. *God.* Did that sound like a come on?

She changed the subject hastily. "Do you have a phone next to your toilet too?"

He laughed. "Yes, but I'm not calling from that phone."

"Oh. Good."

"Yeah." Alec responded with another short laugh. "Are you interested in dinner?"

"I am pretty hungry. What time is our flight out in the morning?"

"Early. Eight, maybe? So, dinner out?"

"Sounds great," she said, pulling the towel tightly across her body.

"Does your sister want to join us?" Alec asked.

"She went back to D.C. I dropped her at Grand Central."

"Excellent," Alec said.

Kate's heart rate kicked up another notch.

They made arrangements to meet in a half-hour.

Kate hung up and attempted to quell the jitters. *Geez. Relax. It's just dinner.*

She wasn't quite ready when he knocked at her door, but she opened it. There he stood, so good-looking in navy pants and a white shirt, he made her mouth water.

What would he do if she grabbed his shirt and yanked him into her room? She thought about what it would be like to lose her virginity to him. It was probably akin to getting your learner's permit, then climbing behind the wheel of a Porsche to cruise the Autobahn. She indulged the fantasy. She'd have to climb him like a tree, since he was almost a foot taller than her. She imagined trying to wrestle his mouth down to hers, licking his lips apart and meeting his tongue. Arousal burned through her, thickening her blood, bringing heat rolling through her body.

He still stood in the doorway, looking puzzled.

Crap. How long had she been staring at him? He was probably accustomed to women lusting over him. Doubtless he had fought off overeager fans and groupies many times. She mumbled something about putting on her shoes and escaped into the bedroom.

*

Alec watched the graceful sway of her hips as she walked into the bedroom and shut the door. There was something disturbingly sexy and quietly innocent about Kate. And then there was that black number she was wearing. She had a hot body. And that dress clung to every curve. He wanted to grab her arms, hold them over her head and have her turn slowly in front of him so he could see the slopes, the dips, and valleys.

What was this odd combination of lust and tenderness she stirred in him? Was she even aware of his X-rated thoughts? She certainly kept him at arm's length. Ever since that morning of the rescue she had played a starring role in most of his fantasies. Siren Kate, with her soulful, green eyes and masses of unruly, thick red wavy hair. What would she do if he pushed his way into the room, and kissed and stroked her until she let him deep into her warm, wet body? Arousal swept through him and he glanced down. He was rock hard. What the hell was that? She was not his type. She wasn't, right? He felt the blood rush through him as he closed his eyes, took a deep breath, and sighed. He needed to get her out of this room before he did something he desperately wanted.

They walked to an exclusive restaurant a few blocks from the hotel. Two leisurely hours later, he pushed back from the table. Had she noticed he couldn't keep his eyes off her over dinner? Her body, her looks, her quick wit, everything about her captivated him. She laughed through his anecdotes about traveling and playing overseas, and told a few uproariously funny stories about working as a nurse. Funny and hot. A pretty fantastic combination, if only she weren't so young. Besides, she wasn't his type. Not his type.

The evening air had turned brisk while they were in the restaurant so he helped her into her jacket on the street.

"It's a nice night. Would you like to take the long way back?" he asked.

"Sure."

They had only made it a few blocks but he was so attuned to her, he noticed the faint hitch in her stride. He'd been out with enough women to know the combination of high heels and city streets could be lethal.

"Let's grab a drink somewhere," he said, not ready for the evening to end.

Behind them was a bar advertising karaoke every night. She pointed to the sign hopefully and he shook his head. *No way.* She grabbed his hand, a sly smile on her face and dragged him into the bar. They sat at a table and a waiter with a bored air approached them.

"I'm a little fuzzy from the wine with dinner." She smiled. "I'll have a soda."

"Two Cokes," he said to the waiter.

"Is this okay? Are you comfortable in bars?" she asked, her face registering concern.

"Not a problem." He leaned back in the chair. Bars didn't bother him, not anymore. He took a lot of meetings in bars and restaurants. Being around a bunch of idiots using? That was a different story. He still went out of his way to avoid situations like that.

The drunken joker on stage tortured them with a rendition of 'New York, New York'—then finished the song and wobbled off stage.

Kate rose and held out her hand. "Sing with me."

"Hell, no."

"Suit yourself." With a grin she backed away, moving toward the stage.

"Are you going to?"

Her grin widened. "This is my new leaf, Alec. Our little adventure knocked some sense into me. I'm going to do the things I've always wanted to do."

"Don't you think you're kinda young for a bucket list, Kate?"

She laughed but backed up another step, arm extended again, fear mingling with hope in her eyes.

He pointed at the stage. "Does that scare you?"

She stopped, wide-eyed and nodding. "Of course it does. No sane person sings in public."

He pretended to take offense, raising his eyebrows and ducking his chin.

"C'mon. Show me the ropes." Her eyes sparkled with excitement.

He glanced around. There were no more than two-dozen people in the place, and only a handful in the back near the karaoke machine and stage.

"Really? I haven't sung publicly in ten years and this is where I'm staging my comeback?" he grumbled, rising.

She waited, head cocked, hand extended.

He took her hand and helped her onto the tiny stage.

They flipped through the songs. He couldn't help teasing her about her musical tastes. They were atrocious. She insulted his right back and settled on a Gloria Gaynor song. He picked a recent Spade song which nicely encapsulated the life of a rock star.

"Perfect," she said when he pointed to it. "I programmed my cell to play that when you call," she blurted out, smiling when his jaw dropped. He was ridiculously pleased to hear that. His own ringtone.

"Ladies first."

"No! Please. Age before beauty." Her eyes pleaded with him.

"You sure you want to follow this act?" he purred, gesturing to himself while he stripped off his jacket.

He couldn't believe he had butterflies. In a karaoke bar. He shook his head then picked up the microphone. He didn't need the words on the screen. By the second verse, he was transported back to that familiar place. Excitement and adrenaline surging through him. The sheer joy of belting out the song.

God, how he had missed this.

He was only performing for one person, but it could have been a stadium full of people and he would have felt the same way. He grinned at Kate as she danced, her arms linked above her head, swaying, lost in the music. Turning round, her hips teased him as her lithe body twisted sinuously and her lush mouth shaped the words. Others in the bar had joined in, shouting out the infectious chorus. Typical Spade song.

He put down the microphone, energized, excited and happy. More than that. It had always been this way. How could he have forgotten?

Kate's expression reflected his mood. The shouts, cheers and catcalls from the other patrons finally sank in. One guy in the back held up the image of a lit lighter on his cell phone. Alec bowed, laughing.

Stepping down in front of Kate he gestured to the stage indicating her turn, grinning hugely. The noise in the bar had risen exponentially.

She pulled his head down and said, sobering, "There is no way I can follow that performance."

She leaned back, wide-eyed.

"How 'bout I sing it with you?"

"You'd do that?" Her eyebrows arched. "Really? *That* song?"

They each picked up a microphone. Once the audience heard the opening bars, there was a collective groan from the patrons. Alec started singing. Kate followed his lead. This time, they were nearly booed off stage. Before they were halfway through the song she was bent in half, incapacitated by laughter. Since she was unable to get out most of the lyrics, he covered for her, maintaining his professional aplomb throughout. He grinned, watching her laugh herself silly.

"Your turn," she said wheezing when the song finally ended. She wiped a hand over streaming eyes and put down her microphone. "I don't think the rock star life is for me."

To his surprise and her obvious pleasure, he agreed to sing another song, then another. People at the bar shouted requests at him.

*

Two hours later, Kate and Alec exited the bar. Kate ran a hand still shaking with exhaustion and excitement through her disheveled hair. *What a night.* She carried her shoes, toes too sore to put them back on, even for the short walk from the bar to the cab.

She stared at him as he tried to catch the attention of a taxi driver. He had been transformed up there into someone larger than life. Why on earth was this incredibly talented, sexy, guy practicing law?

He finally hailed a cab, opened the door and gestured for her to precede him into the rear seat.

She couldn't take her eyes off him, mesmerized. "Alec, you were awesome."

He grinned and shifted in the seat.

"No, seriously. You came alive back there. It was amazing."

The cab stopped abruptly and threw them forward. The driver cursed at a car he had barely missed. Kate and Alec shared a glance and something moved between them. Kate turned toward him, somehow in motion, sliding across the imitation leather of the bench seat. Alec's hands came up, met her torso and yanked her into his arms so quickly and efficiently the next thing she knew she straddled him, her dress hiked up to her hips. His hand reached up and gripped the back of her head. He leaned in, licking his way inside her mouth, devouring her.

He dragged his lips across hers, changing the angle, teasing one moment then hard, rough, and deep the next. He used his other hand to press her hips down tightly against his. It should have been uncomfortable, awkward, kissing in the back of a moving cab, instead it felt natural. She melted into him.

It wasn't as though she had never been kissed. But this, this, was far beyond her experience. Beyond her comprehension. The feel of his big warm hands through her dress, the scrape of his jaw against her skin, her cheeks, her neck, increased her arousal until it was a hard, painful insistent ache. It was the most erotic thing she had ever experienced. The movement of the cab only added to the magic.

She moaned. Lust mingled with frustration, muffled by his mouth. His grip on her hips tightened and she became aware of his raging erection, as it pressed, almost painfully, against the thin, now damp barrier of her panties. Kate squirmed, pushed down with her hips, wild to get closer. She ran her hands down the front of his chest, over hot, hard muscles, the ridges of his abdomen, and lower until his hands met hers at his zipper. She pulled back, startled, then met his gaze and felt a momentary panic. His face was all hard planes and intensity, flushed with desire, his blue eyes ablaze with passion.

She might have said something, might have ended it, but he yanked her into him with a growl. Her whole body was swept away with sensation, pliant, aching, boneless. Her hands slid up and found their way into his thick, satiny, gloriously too long hair.

He moved her dress down, over her shoulders, his fingertips rough against her heated skin. She shuddered, barely aware of the downward path of the zipper in back, as he kissed, licked and sucked his way down her neck and collarbone.

Her hands tightened in his hair, urging him on, down further, to her breasts where he sucked and bit at them through the lace mesh of her black bra. She opened her eyes and watched his mouth and tongue against her bra-covered breasts and ground herself down against his erection, mindlessly trying to get closer, wanting more. The pleasure was shocking, dizzying.

Some distant part of her recognized she was out of control. Hell, *they* were out of control. She could feel tremors wrack him and heard his panting breaths. He reached between her legs.

She froze.

She pushed his hands away, frantically. He lifted his head, looked into her eyes and groaned, moving his hands away.

Kate scrambled off him, mortified, unable to make eye contact with Alec or the cab driver who stared at them in the rear view mirror. The cab had stopped. How long had they been sitting in front of the hotel? Squelching hysteria, she pulled the door handle, scrambled onto the sidewalk and dashed past the bellhop a few feet away.

He winked at her.

Oh my God.

Ducking her head, she made for the hotel lobby and elevator, dress still partially unzipped. She clenched the material tightly under her arms to keep it on. She took a panicked step toward the stairs at the end of the lobby, just then the elevator dinged its arrival. Heart racing, key card in hand, she rushed in and pushed her floor. The doors were half closed when a white shirt-clad arm thrust between them. She shrank back into the farthest corner, stared at the number panel and bit her lip. She felt rather than saw him look at her as he entered.

"Kate." Alec's voice was still husky from arousal.

She peered at him through tousled hair.

"I take it you don't want to continue this upstairs?" His tone was matter-of-fact.

A wave of mortification rose and crested, scorching her neck and face. "N-no."

They rode up the rest of the way in silence. He walked her to her room and she said a quiet goodnight. After she closed the door, she slid down onto the carpet.

A rap made her jump.

"Don't forget to lock the top," he said.

"Thanks," she said, weakly.

God. What had she been thinking? Clearly she hadn't. He would probably return to his room and call one of the brunettes from the airport. Or both. Or a supermodel. Whoever. Anyone but her. He was definitely not the person to risk her heart with.

Chapter 9

Alec was grateful she hadn't brought up the previous evening's antics on the flight back. He spent most of the time in the car, at the airport, and during the flight conducting business—on the phone and computer. Kate was polite, but distant. He could tell she was still mortified, obviously uncomfortable around him. She studiously avoided all eye contact.

What had he been thinking? He knew his way around women, but he'd never lost control like that before. What was it about her, this girl, that made her so different from the others?

She buried herself in her e-reader for a few hours, before falling fast asleep. She hadn't reclined the seat so he moved his laptop into the seat pocket and leaned over to do it for her. As he straightened, he got a whiff of her intoxicating scent—something fresh and floral. Images of the previous evening in the cab flashed before him and he felt himself harden. Stunned, he sat the rest of the way back in his seat, staring down at his lap in disbelief. That was the second time in two days! She wasn't even his type. Not at all. He didn't go for short, pale, redheads. Apparently his body hadn't gotten the message. She was beautiful in her own way, but without a hint of glamour or sophistication. He wasn't interested in her. But if that were true, what the hell happened last night?

Kate was…fun. Happy. Down to earth. And here he was, next to her, fully aroused, the day after he'd lost his freaking mind with her in the back of a cab in Manhattan. Bizarre. Maybe he was experiencing an early mid-life crisis.

She said good-bye at the airport as she left for her connecting flight to Cielito, still barely making eye contact. A strange combination of relief mixed with pique swept through him.

Apparently, she wanted nothing to do with him. He took a car from the Los Angeles airport home.

As he unpacked his bag, his cell rang. He smiled at the familiar number. Asher Lowe. Rock star, lead singer and front man for Spade and his best friend since they had started out in the LA music scene all those years ago.

"Ash."

"What the fuck, man?" The voice on the other end of the line was indignant.

Alec frowned. "What?"

"It's bad enough you don't call when you do something heroic …"

"Yeah, yeah. Like you care."

"You wound me, man."

Alec laughed.

"But this?" Asher said.

"Dude. I have no idea what you're talking about. My flight just landed."

"My inbox is full. There's a video circulating of you singing my song at a karaoke bar."

Alec froze, dirty laundry in hand. So much for not wanting the media back in his life. There would be speculation about his performance for weeks. He had no idea anyone had recorded him last night. But of course they had. Everyone had video capability on his or her cell phone these days. He looked heavenward and gave a short laugh.

"And who is the smokin' hot chick with you? She is not your usual type," Asher said. "Are you back in, dude? Cause I got first dibs if you are. I'd give my right arm to collaborate with you."

"That was the extent of my comeback for now, but why don't we meet for lunch or something later in the week. I've been considering other options lately."

"Other options?" Asher's tone was sharp. "Don't tease me. Are you getting back in?"

"Asher, I have so much going on right now at this rate I'll never get to Cielito. Let's get together later in the week. I'll be in town Thursday."

"Shit. I'm out of town Thursday. Promoting in Japan all week. The week after, okay?"

"You know you're always welcome in Cielito."

Asher sighed. "Tell you what, I'll spend a few days there at the end of the month. I should be able to wrap up this promotional stuff by then. We head back into the studio after the first of the year."

*

Five days after the rescue, Kate strode out of the hospital, searching her bag for her cell phone. She pulled it out and checked the face. Two missed calls from her sister.

What now?

She wished Emma would just call to chat, but lately the only time she called was when she needed something, and that something was usually money. Maybe Kate would call back after she'd slept. It would take energy to deal with her sister. Energy she didn't have after all these twelve-hour night shifts. If nursing were this tough three years out of college, she could only imagine how hard it would be in twenty or thirty years. And it wasn't only the effect on the rest of her life. Work had been crazy since she had come back from New York. They had been inundated with patients on her floor and the night shift was not well equipped to handle it.

Craig Billingsly, M.D., cardiothoracic surgeon, leaned against the door to her car.

She halted mid-stride, the air leaving her lungs in a whoosh. "Dr. Billingsly," she said.

"Please, call me Craig." His eyes twinkled. "We're barely on hospital grounds."

Just yesterday she passed a new billboard with his giant, handsome face promoting Cielito Community Hospital and touting his experience. The public relations department was determined to milk his impeccable credentials and reputation for excellence in surgery for all it was worth. Heart patients were coming in droves, some from hundreds of miles away.

"I was hoping you'd join me for dinner Saturday night. I checked the schedule. You're off."

Her palms were sweating. She took a deep breath. She'd promised Ava she'd try. And he'd been really nice and collegial last week when he sat with her in the cafeteria. His insights on nursing care for his post-op cardiac patients were invaluable. She really didn't want to date people she worked with, but where else was she supposed to meet guys?

Take risks. This guy *had* to be a safer bet than Alec Sawyer.

"Sure. I'd love to."

Shivering in the crisp morning air, she hugged herself. She hadn't thought to change out of her scrubs or grab a jacket from her locker.

He beamed at her. "Terrific. Pick you up at six-thirty? We'll have dinner at Chez Henri."

"Great."

He raised a hand and walked by her toward the hospital, the strong odor of his woodsy scent lingering in the early morning air. He sure did lather on the cologne.

Chapter 10

Her doorbell rang at six-thirty exactly. Kate stroked up the nape of her neck, checking her chignon. She hoped she was dressed appropriately for Chez Henri on a Saturday night. She smoothed the little scarlet dress over her hips, grabbed her only clutch and opened the door.

His eyes widened appreciatively. "You look beautiful."

"Thanks." She licked her lips nervously and noticed his gaze lingered at her mouth.

"Nice car." Parked in the curve of the driveway was a shining ebony beast of a Mercedes.

"That thing? It's nothing. My actual car is being serviced, so I got a loaner from the dealer."

Locking the door to the cottage, she tottered the few steps to where he held the door of the black sedan open for her. This was a real date. She gave him points for helping her into the car. Help she could use in a tight fitting dress and four inch heels.

"So, Craig." It felt weird to call him that. "I don't know anything about you. Are you from around here?"

"No," he said. "Alabama." He steered the big black car onto the street.

She moved back in her seat to examine him. "Alabama? You don't have an accent."

"I got rid of it. Accents make you sound ignorant."

She pressed her lips together and shook her head. "I don't think so."

He glanced over at her and sighed. "Let's get the trivial stuff out of the way, shall we? My father was a minister. Very, what's the term he would use? Strict. My mother had eight children with him. Well, there *were* eight of us. My older brother drowned in a flash flood when we were kids."

Kate stared at him, awash in mixture of horror and sympathy. "Gosh. I'm so sorry. I…I don't know what to say. How horrible for you and your family."

He shrugged. "It's in the past. I got out of that podunk town as fast as I could. Never looked back. Don't like to talk about it." He sent her a smile, teeth gleaming in the dark car.

Kate twisted her hands together in her lap. It must be his cologne that was making her slightly nauseous. Or that harrowing childhood experience. "Still—"

"I don't like to talk about that stuff, if that's okay with you."

"Sure," she murmured. "So, do you like Chez Henri?"

"Eh. It's okay, considering the limited options in town."

"Oh, good."

This was so much more awkward than she imagined. And she'd imagined it would be pretty damn awkward. They lucked out with a parking spot right in front. Craig helped her out of the car and held the door on their way into the restaurant. He gave his name to the man at the podium.

"It'll be a few minutes. Would you care to wait at the bar?"

"Certainly," Craig said.

Kate settled herself onto a barstool.

"What'll you have?" the bartender asked.

Craig looked at Kate in askance.

"I'll have a glass of Pinot Noir," Kate said.

" River Myst Haven?" the man asked.

"Perfect," Kate replied.

"And you, sir?"

"A margarita, rocks, with your finest tequila. No salt," Craig said.

Craig asked her some questions about her family. He'd seen the interview on the morning show, so he knew she'd lost her mom to cancer. He was attentive and curious as he asked about her struggles as a hybrid sister-and-mother.

Before she knew it, she was opening up to him about her desire to travel.

"Oh, Kate. Traveling outside the United States sounds wonderful, but in reality it's a major headache. You can't imagine the inconveniences, even in Europe. They don't use the same currency; the outlets require converters and a host of other horrors." He shuddered. "I loathe foreign travel."

She deflated.

He pulled his phone out of his pants pocket. Kate glanced at it. What was that on the face of it? A bright red background? He held up his index finger to her and put the phone to his ear. The maître d' came over to let them know their table was ready. He got the finger too. The man's lips curled into a sneer, but he waited, tapping the menus in his hand. Kate took a healthy swallow of her wine.

Craig spat out a few directives about the patient to whoever was on the other end and disconnected the call after the longest minute of Kate's life.

"Hospital," he said. Rising from the stool, he took her arm. "Shall we follow this gentleman?"

Muted earth tones, dim lighting and the quiet murmur of conversation gave the restaurant a romantic feel. Kate had been there before, special occasions, dinners with the Morgans, celebrations with Emma. It was a treat to go to Chez Henri.

"So, which hospital did you practice at before coming to Cielito?"

His lips twisted and he adjusted his collar. "I thought we weren't going to talk about the past."

Kate blinked. *Geez.* What was he, in witness protection?

With a forced smile, Kate steered the conversation to work. By the time their food arrived, she was seriously annoyed. The attentive guy from the bar was gone. Craig had typed out no fewer than four text messages. He had barely put his phone down, even to order.

The food arrived and Kate waited, fork poised over her entrée, for him to put the phone away. With a sigh, he put it on the table, within arm's reach. Squinting at the phone, she tried to make out the crimson background. Was that a photo?

During dinner he picked up the phone every time it vibrated and tapped out messages. Kate attempted, and failed, to carry the conversation. If he said, 'now, where were we?' one more time she would scream.

The waiter cleared the entrees.

"More wine?"

"No, thanks," Kate answered.

"Another drink, sir?"

"Yes. And wheel the dessert cart over." He winked at Kate. "I know how you gals love the sweets."

Kate cringed.

He typed out yet another message on his phone.

The desert cart arrived at the table. The waiter explained each one, pointing them out with flourish. Craig craned his body over the tray. "Let's have one of each."

Kate's eyes widened and she sat back. One of *each*? There were six desserts on the cart. And this guy was a cardiologist. "None for me, thanks."

His eyebrows rose. "Two forks," he said to the waiter as if she hadn't spoken.

Kate frowned, holding both hands up. "No, really. I'm good."

She met the waiter's amused gaze and narrowed her eyes.

Craig waved at her with his fork. "Dig in. You ladies always say you don't want dessert but as soon as it arrives you scarf it down," he said, through a mouthful of cheesecake.

He pushed the chocolate torte over toward her.

She pushed it back.

"No. The meal was huge and the wine. I can't. Really."

Craig shrugged.

He finished the cheesecake and started on the passion fruit-mango mousse cake. She watched dumbfounded as he made short work of it, finishing in three bites.

She glanced around the restaurant.

He reached for the crème brûlée. At the rate he was shoveling in desserts, he would finish them all in short order.

"Are you on call?" Kate finally asked, nodding at the phone as he finally put down the fork to tap out yet another message.

"What? Uh, no." He glanced up, then looked past her. His eyes lit up.

"Will you excuse me? I see Mark Cass leaving with his wife and I need to speak with him a moment."

Kate froze. Dr. Cass? She did *not* want someone from the hospital to see her with Craig Billingsly. God knows what the rumor mill would do with it and there was no likelihood of second date.

Craig stood, put his cell phone down on the middle of the table with a murmured apology, and took off after Dr. Cass.

She stared at the phone. Now it was close enough to see, and she wished it weren't. Who kept the picture of a live human heart as the background of their phone?

Gross.

The phone vibrated.

She tried not to peek, but it was too tempting.

Eyes wide, she leaned over a smidge to read the incoming text message from someone saved into his phone as 'Kelly'.

Free 2nite?

Kate sat back. The phone vibrated again. Another incoming message popped up on the screen below the first. A photo. A photo of 'Kelly', in a black merry widow, holding a crop. Against the backdrop of the bloody heart. Her stomach clenched.

She chanced a look over her shoulder. From the body language of all involved, it didn't seem like the conversation with Dr. Cass was going all that well. Arms waving, bodies rigid as they discussed something she was too far away to hear. Mrs. Cass, the only one facing her directly, appeared incensed.

The phone vibrated again. This text was from 'Bitch' and it said:

Stop texting me! Contact thru lawyer only.

Kate sat up straight in her chair. Bitch? His ex-wife perhaps? And who was Kelly? The hairs on the back of her neck stood up. Kelly looked vaguely familiar. Was she a nurse at the hospital?

The waiter came over to see if she wanted another glass of wine. "No, thanks."

"Another dessert then, ma'am?"

Kate gave him a disdainful look. He smiled and glanced down at the phone on the table. Her body tensed as the waiters' eyes widened. He glanced at Kate, then back at the phone. She felt a wave of heat rise up through her neck into her face. She averted her gaze. The man made a choked sound and strode away.

Craig reappeared at her side.

She studiously avoided looking at the phone, watching out of her peripheral vision as he slid it off the table into his hand.

Stomach in knots, Kate debated her options. Should she tell him she saw the messages? It was snooping and she didn't want to get in a big discussion about it with him getting defensive or lying or whatever.

She took the easy way out.

"Listen, thanks so much for dinner. It was great. I, um, really appreciate it. Really. I had some reservations before, since we work together and I, I …" She took a deep breath, "I've come to realize I don't want to date someone I work with."

What had been a polite, expectant expression morphed into surprise then anger flashed in his eyes. A nanosecond later, the anger was banked and his expression turned pleading, his large blue eyes wide, he held a hand out to her, and leaned forward.

"Kate. Don't worry about work. They're desperate to keep me." His phone buzzed on the table next to him. Once, then again. He seemed oblivious.

Kate leaned back, pressing her lips together. "No, I get that. It's just that *I'm* not comfortable. The gossip. I'm just, it's not…. so, thanks for dinner." She rose, putting her napkin on the table, grabbing her purse. She stumbled over the chair leg of a neighboring table. "Excuse me. Sorry."

Heart racing, she pushed through the restaurant door and out onto the street. Hampered by the tight skirt and unaccustomed to high heels she teetered, breathless, up a half block before ducking into a store alcove.

Digging through her bag she found her phone and tapped on her contacts, found Ava and pressed the button.

"Ava?"

"Kate? I can barely hear you!" Ava shouted.

"Where are you?"

"Whaaat? Hold on. Let me get somewhere quieter…..okay…. what's up?"

"Where are you?" Kate hissed.

"I'm at Agave. Hey, aren't you supposed to be on a date?"

"I'm coming to you; I'll be there in ten," Kate said, disconnecting the phone.

She peered out of the alcove. He was probably still paying the check or finishing dessert. Crossing over to the other side of the street, she hustled the four blocks to Ava's favorite bar.

Her friend was standing by the entrance, lemon drop martini in hand when Kate walked in.

Ava stared, then gave a low wolf-whistle, handing over the drink.

Kate took one sip, then a second, then downed it while Ava watched, eyes huge.

"Whoa, girlfriend! You're running tomorrow."

Ava took the glass back, put it on the bar next to her and steered Kate toward the quieter of the two lounges. She parked Kate on the crimson velveteen sofa and fell onto the cushion beside her.

Ava leaned toward her. "So?"

Kate told her about the date. Now that she was away from Craig Billingsly, the whole thing seemed funny, in a horrible kind of way.

Ava drew back, shaking her head, laughing. "Oh, Kate. You sure can pick 'em. Are you sure it was a human heart?"

Kate nodded, wide-eyed. "I guess I should thank my lucky stars he wasn't a proctologist."

"A whaaa?"

"Never mind." Kate shook her head, glumly. "Hopefully it won't be too awkward at work. I don't run into him much."

"You want to stay here?" Ava checked her watch.

"Hell, no. I want a ride home."

Ava sighed and glanced around the bar. "Not much talent here tonight, anyway. And I'm running the tent at the five-K race at the crack of dawn tomorrow."

"Good. I'll see you after."

Minutes later Ava pulled into her driveway. Kate reached for the door handle. "I've been meaning to tell you, I hooked up with Alec Sawyer in New York."

Ava stared at her in the dark car, open-mouthed. "Did you—"

She laughed. "No. Not that. We just kissed—there may have been some groping."

"And?"

"And nothing. I came to my senses. I realized I was playing with fire, thank God."

"Fire? So it was good."

The heat rose in her cheeks and Kate looked away.

"Goddamn it. Why didn't you tell me? Are you going to see him again?"

"No."

"Why not?"

She blew out a breath. "Ava, he is so far—"

"If you say 'out of my league' I'm going to throttle you. Fair warning."

Kate rubbed a hand over her tired eyes. "Can we talk about this later?"

"No. I know you think he's hot—"

"Yes. He's gorgeous. And smart and funny and sweet. And women shove their phone numbers in his pockets at airports. And he dates women who look like super-models. Heck, they probably *are* super-models."

Ava reached out a hand and took Kate's. "If you like him, you can't hold that stuff against him."

"I know. It doesn't matter anyway. We were both embarrassed by what happened."

"How'd you leave it?"

"He wanted to take it further that night. I didn't. He was cool about it. But the flight back sure was awkward. Okay." Kate reached across to give her friend a hug, difficult in the confines of Ava's sub-compact car, then opened the door and stepped out.

"See you tomorrow at the run. And Kate?"

"Yes?" Kate leaned in the car door.

"Promise me you'll give Alec a chance if it comes to that?"

"After tonight's experience? Ha!"

"Promise!"

"'Night, Ava." She shut the door with a grin, walked up the path and let herself in to her silent cottage.

Chapter 11

It had been a week since the rescue. Back in Cielito for the past two days, Alec looked for her every morning while he surfed. This morning the ocean was laughably flat. No one in their right mind would be out trying to surf an ocean that was lake-like in its calm. He sat astride his board, the early morning sun reflecting off the blue sea. If he did see Kate this morning, what explanation could he give for being out in such poor conditions? Why didn't he call her? This attempt to bump into her was a bust and he couldn't put off his meetings in LA tomorrow.

He spotted her then. Running. Loose red hair gleaming in the morning light, neon pink shoes in motion. His heart gave a leap. Even at this distance, he could see when she spotted him. He put a hand up, she waved in response. Turning his board toward shore he lay down, paddling hard.

"Morning." He pulled his board from the water as she ran up.

"Hi." She stopped, breathing hard. "I was hoping to see you. Doug Curley was discharged two days ago."

"That's awesome."

"Yeah. He wants to thank you in person. I have his info at home," she said, staring down at her feet.

"Yeah, yeah. Of course." He nodded. "Do you have time to grab breakfast or something? I can get his info from you then."

She hesitated. Her enchanting green eyes met his gaze, her face flushed, hairline damp. "Uh, okay," she said.

There it was again, that little hitch in his chest. Odd. He usually felt lust a little lower.

"Want me to swing by after I clean up?" he asked.

"I'll be ready." She ran backwards for a moment, gave him a dazzling smile and headed back down the beach.

*

Almost two hours later, Kate watched Alec across the table on the patio of the sidewalk café, breakfast devoured, leisurely enjoying coffee and people watching. Hard to believe she could be so comfortable casually chatting with the guy she had jumped in a cab. He was funny and easy to talk to, just like he had been over dinner in New York. There was something about him. Granted, he was charming – charismatic even, but he had a sincerity about him. She'd been around charming men and distrusted them and she'd be willing to bet her father was charming. But instead of recoiling from him, she found herself falling further and further into the soft comfort of his voice.

What had Ava told her? Not to hold stuff against him that he couldn't control?

A familiar face in a hooded sweatshirt and board shorts appeared, whizzing down the sidewalk on a skateboard in front of them.

He caught her eye and did a double take. "Kate!"

"Buzz. I haven't seen you in ages."

Buzz picked up his skateboard and clambered over the railing.

He leaned over to give her a hug. His lips puckered and Kate quickly averted her mouth, taking the kiss on the cheek. She shook her head. He hadn't changed since high school. He pulled up a chair from a neighboring table; the smell of patchouli emanating from him widened her smile.

Kate introduced the two men. "I went to high school with Buzz. He works at Pizzatown and does some contracting jobs for a friends company. Buzz, this is Alec Sawyer—"

"Yeah. I know who he is. Big fan, man. I heard you lived in town."

The men chatted a few minutes, discussing everything from construction in the area to the coming swell generated by storms raging in the Pacific.

"So Alec, any chance you'll get back in the biz?" Buzz played air guitar over the table.

Alec shook his head. "Nah. I just represent the talent now."

As they talked, she watched a convertible red Mercedes pull into a metered parking spot across the street. The occupant didn't emerge. Mercedes were a dime a dozen in this town, but lately she had been seeing that particular one everywhere, on her street, in town. The personalized plate read FIXNHRT. Fixing hurt? Maybe a therapist or psychiatrist. Strange what people put on their license plates.

Kate sipped her coffee. Pleasantly exhausted from her run and her shift, she lacked the energy to feel nervous or awkward with Alec. Her phone vibrated. She pulled it out and checked the number. Billingsly. She turned it off and stuffed it back in her pocket, frowning. Ever since that bad date, he had been leaving voicemails and sending text messages. The message he left last night was really over the top. How he could give her everything she could ever want, she just had to give him a chance. Was there a way to block his calls and texts? Ignoring him didn't seem to be working.

"Kate, you ok?" asked Alec.

"Yeah, sorry, yeah," she said, and Alec smiled, and turned back to Buzz.

She cast a surreptitious glance Alec's way. God he was sexy. She must have relived that incident in the cab a hundred times since returning to Cielito. To make matters worse, he played a starring role in each and every one of her fantasies. He'd even crept his way into her dreams. She watched his beautiful mouth as he spoke to Buzz. Perfectly shaped lower lip, slightly fuller than the upper, quirked in an amused half smile as he listened to Buzz. It was impossible to see that mouth and not remember how it had stroked her own. Her fingers touched her lips reflexively. Alec's gaze caught and held hers and the heat of arousal mixed with embarrassment crept over her. His smile turned knowing. She looked away.

He turned back to his conversation with her friend and she resumed her study of his features. Presumably he always had that five o'clock shadow, highlighting a strong jaw and enviable cheekbones. Even right after he had shaved, leaving for their appearance on the morning programs in New York, his beard was evident. Most men with that much scruff on their face were hairy everywhere. Not him, his arms only had a smattering of hair. It took her a moment to realize that deep-set, intense, bright-blue eyes were watching her with amusement, corners creased with laugh lines.

Dropping her gaze to his hands, she watched the long elegant fingers of his left hand flip and toy with a spoon. What was with his fingertips? She had seen a lot of deformities in the hospital. Advanced lung or heart disease often caused the fingers past the last joint to become rounded and bulbous or "clubbed". That was not clubbing. She leaned closer, puzzled. He was giving his full attention to whatever Buzz was saying.

She studied his other hand resting on the table, the one without the spoon. No, the tips of his left hand were callused, but not the right. Now why would that be? She was on the verge of asking him about it when it came to her. Those were calluses from playing guitar. She gasped and both men turned to her. She covered the gasp with a cough and averted her gaze toward the street. He told her on the airplane that he didn't play anymore. Hell, he'd just denied it to Buzz.

What a whopper!

A tall, thin blonde in a blue micro-mini, yellow fleece hooded sweatshirt, and tan Ugg boots clomped down the sidewalk.

The woman noticed Buzz and froze. Even from this distance, Kate could see her eyes widen and her face contort into a mask of rage. She stormed over, marching through the gate toward their table.

"Uh oh," Kate whispered to Alec. He followed her gaze, sitting back in his chair.

"Madison!" Buzz greeted her with a shout of happy recognition, oblivious to what was so clearly written on her face. Kate and Alec exchanged wide-eyed looks. Her figure taut with thinly suppressed animosity, she strode to where they sat.

"You son-of-a-*bitch*," she hissed at Buzz, eliciting curious stares from other patrons at the café.

"Babe," Buzz sounded hurt, "what the hell? I haven't had a chance to call--"

"You didn't tell me you lost the condom last night!"

"Whaaaa?" He was either too stoned or too clueless to catch her meaning.

"Last night? You failed to mention that your condom came off?" She was spitting fury. All other conversation on the patio died down. All eyes turned to the spectacle.

Slowly the light dawned for Buzz. "Yeah," he said, stroking his chin. "It did come off. Wonder what happened to it?"

Kate was caught between horror and hilarity, mouth agape. Even Alec was leaning forward now, studying the couple.

"It was still in me!" she shrieked. "It came out at Zumba this morning!"

A snort of laughter escaped Kate. She clapped a hand over her mouth at the twin expressions of incredulity on the male faces.

Madison turned a scathing look on her.

Alec met Kate's gaze, then he started to laugh, and didn't bother to stifle it.

Madison glared at them both. "So. Not. Funny."

Buzz was the picture of concern and confusion. "Can that even happen?"

"Asshole," she spat and turning on her heel, she fled the patio.

The patio was silent.

"Seriously, Kate, can that even happen?" Buzz asked, shifting in his seat.

She shrugged. "I have no idea."

"I know you don't *really* know, like first hand," Buzz responded. "But, like, as a nurse, have you ever heard of that happening…" he trailed off as Kate shot him an incredulous glare. She could not believe he was alluding to that around Alec.

Alec turned a quizzical expression on her, then turned back to Buzz. Intercepting Alec's look, Buzz said "Dude, I'm not telling you anything you don't already know. Kate doesn't put out. Hell, do you even date anymore, Kate?"

Kate sat stunned. The hot flush of embarrassment crept up her neck and then over her face.

Damn her fair skin.

"I date," Kate replied. Recovering, but still flushed, she turned to Buzz. "Why don't you ask our resident sexpert about disappearing condoms?" she said, gesturing to Alec.

"Damn man, it's never happened to me." Alec laughed, putting his hands up as if to ward off the series of questions he could see Buzz gearing up to ask.

Alec turned a wicked look on Kate, his teeth flashing and his eyes boring into hers. "But then again, condoms are a snug fit for me."

Kate pursed her lips. She refused to laugh.

Buzz was oblivious.

"Later," he muttered, obviously still puzzling over Madison's bombshell, he picked up his skateboard and hopped back over the gate. Kate stood and walked to the sidewalk. She put a hand on his shoulder.

"She's mad Buzz, but there's no injury. Maybe call to apologize?"

He nodded, glum, and took off down the street.

*

Alec watched her standing at the gate. Probably reassuring the guy.

She was, as Asher said, 'smokin' hot'. He studied her from the top of her still-wet, thick curling hair to her pale pink toenails. His groin tightened. So much for hoping her effect on him had diminished.

She returned to the table and sat down.

"So, you don't put out?" He didn't believe it of course. Not for one minute. No one got to twenty-five, looking like she did, and stayed a virgin. Didn't happen. He sat back and played with his spoon, flipping it, eyes on her.

She seemed taken aback, then blushed again. He watched her translucent skin pink up with fascination. *Do I even know anyone who still blushes?* He racked his brain. Nope. It was charming. He enjoyed reading every emotion as it crossed her face. People in his line of work prided themselves on keeping their cards close to their vest. He was surprised and delighted at being able to read what she was thinking in her expressive, green eyes.

She peeked up at him through her lashes and tugged on a strand of her hair. He almost groaned aloud as his body responded.

"He only knew me in high school."

"You didn't have a serious boyfriend in high school?" he asked, idly raising a hand and signaling the waitress for the check. He hadn't meant to stay so long. There was a conference call he couldn't miss in less than an hour.

"Not really. There wasn't a lot of time."

His attention snapped back to her. "Right. Because of your mom and your sister." The smile he directed at her was gentle.

"Well, between that and school and things."

"Hmmm. Yeah, but in college…right?" He watched her. There it was again, the downcast look, the hair tug, that half-embarrassed air he was coming to know.

"Kate?"

She glanced up, eyes wide and guileless. "Well, it was nursing school, which is mostly women…"

He knew his face was registering astonishment.

Her gaze skittered away.

"Since you got out of nursing school?" Even he could hear the pleading is his tone. *Don't let her be a virgin.* Her youth he could deal with, even her relative inexperience, she'd been on an airplane only four times for heaven's sake, but virginity? No fucking way. He had never been with a virgin. Ever. The idea of someone of his experience with a virgin was ludicrous.

"It's not something to be ashamed of," she said, hotly, raising what he now knew were innocent eyes to his.

"I've dated. I just…I just wanted to wait for the right time," she said, softly.

He muffled a groan but she heard it.

She stood. Hands fisted at her sides.

"Sit, please," he said.

She flung herself back into the chair with a scowl as the waitress arrived with the check. Kate pulled out her wallet and tossed money on the table. He ignored the cash, stuffed a black credit card into the plastic tray and shoved it back toward the edge of the table.

He rubbed his hands over his face. He hadn't been able to get her out of his mind since he met her. The incident in the cab fired up his libido and he fantasized about her constantly. Finding out she was inexperienced—no, more than that, a virgin—cooled his ardor. How did he extricate himself from this politely?

When he glanced up, he caught sight of her heading out the patio gate. A hissing breath escaped him and he called her name authoritatively. Patrons on the patio turned to stare at him. He'd be damned if he would give them another sideshow. She didn't stop or turn back.

Damn it!

He pulled the credit card off the table, replaced it with cash and hastened after her.

His long stride ate up the pavement. He grabbed her hand and spun her toward him. Her eyes were so full of tears he doubted she could even see. He felt the bottom drop out of his stomach. *Crap!* Pulling her into an alleyway between buildings lined by plants, he tugged her into his arms.

"I'm sorry."

She sniffled. He held her tightly to him and kissed the top of her head. He had to bend over to do it. How could someone so tiny have so much hair and why did the smell of her send another surge of lust through him?

"I'm an asshole." He squeezed her, arms wrapped tightly around her curvy frame.

She didn't argue.

"I knew you were sheltered," he said. "I didn't realize the extent of it."

She drew back and looked up at him. "I'm not sheltered. No teenager who watches their parent die and assumes the responsibility of a child is sheltered. I'm a virgin."

He grimaced.

"Stop doing that," she growled.

He gave a half-laugh. "What am I doing?"

"Making faces and rude noises!"

Another laugh escaped him and he felt an unexpected surge of tenderness wash through him.

"It's not that crazy. I wanted to wait for the right time and the right person. You try parenting a teenage girl and explaining why you can have sex and she can't. Besides, a lot of guys don't want to date a girl with as much baggage as I have, then or now—"

"I have baggage," he interrupted, "the whole Louis Vuitton set. Trust me, you don't even have a carry-on."

"But I *do* have baggage. And some of it now is this damn virginity," she insisted, eyes peeking up at him through her mass of wavy hair.

He paused for a split second and stared down at her.

He yanked her up, hands cupping the firm swell of her bottom, got her to eye level and pushed her back against the wall, holding her there with his body. Lowering his mouth to hers, he kissed her, fierce, hard. Instant conflagration, just like in the cab. He leaned back and met her smoldering green half-closed eyes. Her arms went around his neck and tugged. Her open mouth pressed eagerly to his. She smelled of flowers and sunshine.

His hands moved up and down her body, fingers stroking her until she moaned her pleasure into his mouth. He moved his hips against her and felt her legs move restlessly against his. One hand went gently under her shirt and pulled her bra cup down until her breast filled his palm. He rolled the nipple lightly between his fingers and she went wild; her tongue lashed his, her thighs wrapped around his hips as she tried to squirm closer, using her legs to pull his hips against her, harder. A low noise rumbled through his throat. Pinching her firmly, she gave a cry of pleasure muffled by his mouth. He fisted a hand in her thick hair and pulled her toward him.

"You make me ache," she whispered against his stroking mouth. His breathing accelerated, the kiss spun out of control.

A police siren shrieked up the street startling him. He pulled back, shocked.

They were in an alley for God's sake.

He gently lowered her feet to the ground and set her from him to pull himself back together. He was shaking. She had never been so alluring.

"God you're beautiful." The words slipped out of him, unbidden.

She smiled shyly. "Well, I guess that answers that question."

"The 'am I willing to take your virginity right now, against this wall' question?" he panted.

She laughed. "I was thinking more along the lines of, is he as attracted to me as I am to him?"

He stared at her, incredulous. "Asked and answered in the back of a cab in New York. The chemistry with you is—"

"Yeah," she interrupted. "It is. But I haven't heard from you."

He laughed. "I've been sitting on my surfboard on a flat ocean hoping to see you for the past two days." His admission startled him in its honesty.

Her eyes widened. "Really? But I only run on workday mornings."

He glanced at his watch and groaned. "I've got a conference call. Can I take you home and call you later?"

"Sure. I'll be sleeping for the next few hours and I have to go in tonight around six."

He frowned. "I have business in LA tomorrow and the next day, but I'll make arrangements to stay in Cielito for a day or two after that. We'll go do something fun."

He slung an arm over her shoulder, pulling her up against his body and they headed for his car.

Chapter 12

A few hours later, humming to herself, she pulled the makings of a salad out of the refrigerator. The cell phone rang. Her heart leapt. Alec?

No. The area code was unfamiliar, so she answered it cautiously. The rescue had been more than a month ago, yet there were still occasional calls from the media. And Billingsly. Always Billingsly. Daily texts. Nightly voicemails. Insisting she give him another chance. At least it wasn't him.

"Kate Gibson?" the masculine voice on the other end of the phone asked.

"Yes?"

"It's your father."

All the blood rushed out of her head and white spots clouded her vision. She slowly sank to the kitchen floor pressing her forehead to folded knees. My God. Him. After all this time. Her mind raced but she sat, utterly still, the rapid throb of her heartbeat deafening.

"Damn it, say something," he demanded.

"How did you get this number?" she croaked.

"Never mind," he said. "Don't you think I had a right to know?"

Rage washed over her clearing out the disconnected feeling and she sat up abruptly. The wooziness counteracted by the heat of fury and adrenaline racing through her bloodstream.

"You don't have a right to anything," she enunciated with finality.

He let out a sharp crack of laughter. "Oh, that's hilarious. I don't have a right to anything? I gave up college. I gave up my career when your mother got pregnant with *you*, and took that dead end fucking job at the bank. I made sacrifices and then you guys kicked me out. So don't tell me I have no right."

Kate sat, speechless. So that's why they got married. Still, how was she to blame? Or her mother for that matter?

He blew out a breath, and when he spoke his tone was calmer, kinder. "Look, that's not what I mean to say. I would've liked to be around to help you. They said on television you raised Emma yourself. How were you able to do that?"

"I was eighteen, the social worker—"

He interrupted. "Did your mother keep that life insurance policy?"

Really? But of course this was about money.

"It's gone. Long gone." Kate lied.

"I don't know what your mother told you, but we didn't have the most amicable parting."

Her fist clenched. "Mom didn't tell me anything. The police reports did."

"Emma is my daughter."

Kate closed her eyes.

"Don't bother to deny it, she looks as much like me as you do."

Kate opened her eyes, body hollow and vaguely nauseated.

"Why wasn't I contacted when your mother died?" His tone was even. "I'm her father, legally you guys had to let me know."

"The birth certificate lists Emma's father as unknown," she replied, woodenly.

It was his turn to be silent. Then he blew up.

"That is *bullshit!* She didn't list me as the *father?* What the hell was wrong with that lying bitch?"

Tears of rage choked her throat. She would not give him the satisfaction. Her heartbeat thundered in her ears but she fought for control and won. She did not dignify his words with a response.

"I want to talk to Emma. Put her on," he ordered.

Through gritted teeth, she replied, "She's unavailable."

"Bullshit. Put her on!"

"No. Don't raise your voice to me and don't call us again," she said, as evenly as she could manage. "Matt, we don't want you in our lives. Leave us alone."

"I want to talk to Emma. I have a right." He disconnected the call.

Kate started at the phone in her hand as though it had turned into a snake. She sat frozen, mind racing, then called Roy Morgan.

By the time the call went through to Roy, she was crying too hard to speak. He tried for a few moments to calm her before he gave up. "Where are you?"

"Home."

"Sit tight. I'll be there in ten minutes. Diana is out but I'll text her."

What felt like a long time later she heard a knock, let Roy in and collapsed in his arms.

He held her away from him. "Has something happened to Emma?" His tanned face was lined with concern.

She shook her head, gestured to her phone and got out "Matt."

"Damn it," Roy said, fingers tightening on her arms. "Don't worry, love. He can't hurt you or Emma." Between hiccoughing breaths she relayed the conversation. "He wants to talk to Emma. He tried to tell me my mom was a lying bitch. I could kill him."

A few minutes later, Diana arrived and took Kate into her arms.

"I'm going to call the police. Give them a heads up," Roy said. "Everyone just calm down. He's probably just gotten himself into trouble again. And he always had a gift for sniffing out money."

"What do I do?" Kate asked, gripping Diana's hand.

"Let's wait and see."

"Come back to our house and we'll have dinner, watch a movie, and relax," Diana said. "We'll figure it out."

Relax? Impossible.

Chapter 13

The door jingled as Alec held it open for Kate to precede him into the kayak shop. The three days since they made out in the alley felt like an eternity. Alec had texted her to set up the date yesterday. She'd been counting the minutes until she could see him again. She debated telling him about the call from her father. No. He dealt with enough of that stuff at work. No way would she burden him with her family issues this early in the relationship.

"We've never done this. What do we need to know?" Alec asked the girl behind the counter while Kate leafed through the brochure.

She looked up to see the cute, young sales girl preening, flipping her hair and peering up at Alec with wide brown eyes as she explained the cold weather gear, cost, timing, and rules of the self-guided excursions into the slough. Alec examined the brochure while Kate watched the sales girl look up at him, her eyes racing over Alec's broad chest and arms, idly chewing one finger while her other hand twisted her bottle-bleached split ends. "Do you want a private guided tour?" she near-whispered to Alec, completely ignoring Kate.

He looked over at Kate with a wide grin. She shook her head and raised her brows.

"No thanks."

"Two person kayak or a kayak for each of you?"

"Two person." he said, definitively.

"Two person?" Kate asked, skeptically. "Why?"

He threw an arm over her shoulders and leered. "I wanna be close."

Even the casual touch sent her heart skipping. She shrugged away, laughing. "That's awfully close, you might capsize us."

He grinned. "Don't you want me to do most of the work?"

"Sure."

They geared up. The girl directed them to the kayak, making a point to walk behind Alec and watch him from behind, but she resumed a more professional approach once Kate glared at her and coughed twice.

Alec took one end of the kayak, Kate the other, and they carried it to the water. It was heavier than it looked and their height difference made it difficult to carry. Kate laughed aloud at the picture they must present.

The girl explained the rules of the slough again, lingering next to Alec. "This is a protected area. Give the wildlife a wide berth. We close in less than four hours so don't get so far out that you can't get it back in time. Be aware the tide is going out and you cannot bring the kayak into the open ocean."

"Got it," Alec said, dismissively.

The girl reluctantly turned back toward the store.

Kate helped Alec push the boat into the murky water. Her white bare feet froze immediately. She narrowly avoided stepping on a jellyfish. With a shriek, she scrambled into the boat.

Behind her he shouted with laughter, but continued pushing until the bottom floated. She turned to watch him hop into the rear seat. Pushing her paddle down to the sandy, muddy bottom, she propelled them farther into the water.

She peered over the side, then drew back with a shudder. "Look at all the jellyfish."

"Mmmm."

She glanced over her shoulder to see him trying to hide a huge grin.

She cocked her head. "Are they in the ocean now?"

"I haven't seen any. They must like this water better. Warmer, right?

Kate adjusted her position on the plastic seat, carefully. "They totally creep me out."

"No. Really? It's funny to see you be such a girl about something."

She turned again to look at him, affronted.

"Where to?"

Kate squinted, peering further into the slough. "I see a raft of sea otters."

Alec gave her some pointers on paddling. Doing it correctly wasn't as simple as it seemed. His technique was far superior to hers.

They drifted over by the otters; the current taking them further into the slough.

Kate tossed a glance at him over her shoulder. "So, tell me about your family."

"My family? Ha. You want to open that can of worms?"

"Uh oh."

"Yeah. My parents were lousy. My dad screwed around on my mom. She didn't seem to care as long as she could shop. She buys stuff constantly." He gave a bitter laugh.

"They sound bad," she admitted "but not—"

"Not awful?"

"Yeah."

"After Bliss became successful, I sent them plenty of money. Lots of money. Apparently it wasn't enough. They sent my brother out to stay with me when I was pretty far gone. He stole a bunch of stuff."

She gasped.

"He stole my checkbook, forged my name, took titles to my vehicles and wrecked some, sold others—"

"Your brother and your parents stole from you?" Her voice rose, incredulous.

"Happens a lot in the business. *Everyone* wants a piece. I'm lucky. Reeking Bliss still pays tremendous royalties, so my parasites, such as they were, didn't make much of a dent, long term. They scavenged maybe a million."

She sucked in a breath, craning her neck to stare back at him. "They stole a million dollars?"

"You have to understand. I was out of it. Really out of it. I had good people in my life, but they were no match for all the bad shit going on. People, substances. And no one cannibalizes like the relatives. I see it all the time."

She rested her paddle across her legs, twisting back to examine him. "I'm sorry. That's terrible."

"Don't feel too bad for me. I was lucky enough to grow up next to the most generous, kind-hearted people in the world, the Thatchers. They did a much better job raising me than my parents did. I've considered myself an honorary Thatcher since I was twelve. Dave Thatcher is still a good friend. He lives in LA near me and still talks to me despite all the bad things that happened. I get dinner with his wife and kids every few weeks. It's good."

He splashed her with the paddle. She gave a low scream and the closest sea otters dove underwater in obvious disapproval.

"Let's go irritate the sea lions over there." He gave a few long pulls with the oar, directing them toward the channel where the current was strongest. She added her efforts.

"Your turn," he said, quietly.

The slough water murky but calm. She paddled aimlessly.

"My mom was an awesome mom, a real class-room volunteering-cookie-baking-all-out-for-the-holidays kind of mom. And tough. You could see that when she got sick." Kate stopped paddling. "Tougher than I thought, actually. After she died, I found out that she was stronger than I ever gave her credit for."

"When did she get sick?"

"She was first diagnosed when I was almost fifteen and Emma was seven, almost eight. She had a routine mammogram and they found a lump. You probably can guess how it went from there. Mastectomy, chemotherapy, remission, but it kept coming back.

She was sick for a long time." She trailed her fingers in the water, then yanked them out.

Jellyfish.

He muttered, "I'm so sorry."

She twisted around and gave him a wan smile.

"We all figured she'd come through it, at first. I remember Roy and Diana used to say—"

"Roy and Diana?"

"Family friends. They helped us a lot those years."

The sea lions on the pier moaned at one another and jockeyed for position. A cold wet sea lion jumped out of the water onto a warm, dry pile of his sleeping brethren. They roared and snapped their displeasure.

"It wasn't as bad as it sounds. I mean it was, but it wasn't, know what I mean? I didn't have much of a social life, but that was okay. After the cancer came back, Mom couldn't really take care of much—from Emma to errands, I was pretty busy."

"You had to grow up fast."

"Yeah. Right up until the end she thought, or at least pretended, it was a fight she could win."

"So she had hope right until the end? Not a bad thing."

"No, but her denial was hard on us. I was barely eighteen and afraid to bring up practical matters about the future without her. There were a lot of things I didn't know that I should have before she died. I had some idea of our finances of course, but there were other issues."

He nodded. "And your dad? Did he come to help?"

Kate took a deep shuddering breath. "No."

When the silence had gone on a while, Alec finally asked, "Why not?"

"He left when I was seven."

"He didn't come take care of you when she died?"

Lost in their discussion, they hadn't notice the current was taking them too close to the small dock at the edge of the slough. They gasped when a sea lion surfaced a foot in front of the kayak. She helped him paddle away and they were silent for a few minutes.

"So?"

Kate pressed her lips together. She was hoping he had forgotten the question.

"We didn't want him to. My mom refused to let me contact him before she died."

"Did your mom tell you why?"

"No."

"Did you ever find out?" he asked.

"Yeah. Diana told me. Well, Diana was with me when Mom's attorney told me."

He gave a long, low whistle.

She turned to look at him. He had stopped paddling. "Yeah. Diana and Aldrich had a file with the divorce paperwork…and other stuff. My father, he is…" she paused. Unsure of what to say or how to say it. She never talked about her father. Why was she telling him? Because he wouldn't be shocked. He'd experienced his own family trauma.

"A deadbeat?" he prompted.

Kate stiffened. "No. A criminal."

"What was in the file?" he asked, sharply.

She groaned inwardly. Of course he would pick up on that. He was an attorney after all.

"Divorce documents, other papers," she hedged.

"And?" he asked.

She could feel his gaze boring into her back. They were drifting in the current now, toward the middle of the slough.

She sat stiffly, paddle across her lap. "Police reports."

He cursed. "Kate, look at me."

She turned, and found his concerned gaze on her.

"Was there abuse?"

She couldn't suppress the quaver in her voice. "My mom was abused. Emotionally throughout, but only physically at the end. She got pregnant the summer after high school and I think he blamed her and me for ruining his chances to finish college."

Kate gazed out over the water, her vision tear-blurred, throat thick. "Diana told me she finally got a restraining order after he threw me across a room. I was trying to separate them."

He sighed. "God, Kate. I'm so, so sorry."

"I had a mild concussion. The police got child protective services involved. My mom got into therapy. There was a restraining order put in place. The Morgans stepped in to help. It's a small town and my dad was persona non grata in it long before…that. Other people came forward, filed charges. Embezzlement, con stuff."

"Good."

"Yes. They threatened my dad with prison if he didn't sign off on the divorce and leave, permanently."

"Aldrich and Diana?"

"No. The chief of police, my mom, pretty much everyone. Diana told me mom was finally done with him. Mom was lucky to have people willing to stick their necks out to get him out of her life. He could have gone to prison but who knows how long he would've been in? He signed the documents and we haven't seen him since. Emma was born after he left."

"He never paid child support, for either of you?"

"No," she paused. "My mom felt that would have given him renewed access to our lives. I elected not to pursue it either."

"I think if you bring a life into this world you should support it."

"You heard the part where I told you he was a psychopath, right?"

"Yeah. But don't you think he should've taken financial responsibility for his children?"

She turned to stare at him.

"We wanted nothing to do with that monster." Splashing her paddle for emphasis. When the paddle broke the surface it sent a stream of water directly at Alec, soaking him. He stared at her, mouth open in disbelief, blinking the salty water out of his eyes. His hair was soaked, rivulets running down his face.

She gasped. "Oh. Oh no. I'm so sorry." She bit the inside of her cheek to keep from laughing, but it wouldn't be stifled. The expression on his face.

He stopped her choked laughter with a splash from his own paddle.

"Hey!" she blurted. "Stop that!"

He splashed her again, and laughing, she flung water back with all of her heart.

*

Alec cranked the heater down. It had taken most of the drive home from the kayak place, but they were finally warm. Damp and disheveled, but warm.

"Can I pick you up for dinner at six-thirty?" Alec asked as he pulled into her driveway, his mind half on the work he had to finish at home before he could see her again.

"Sure." She climbed out of the car, gave him a jaunty wave and rushed down the path to the cottage.

He was on a call for work longer than expected. By the time he called to get reservations, the restaurant had nothing until eight. There was a time he would've used his name to get an earlier spot and boot some unsuspecting patron out of theirs. His lips twisted. Thank God he wasn't that arrogant anymore. He'd be at her place at six-thirty. They could go out and walk around Cielito before dinner.

Hours later, he parked on the circular driveway, got out and followed the path to her little one story cottage next to the main house. Both homes had the Spanish style red tile roofs and the white stucco walls common in Cielito. The large house was huge and, from the look of it, empty.

Alec knocked firmly on the door, casting an idle glance around. Beautifully landscaped.

Kate opened the door and he caught his breath. She had swept up her hair and put on a dark purple dress, which exposed one alabaster shoulder. He glanced down taking in the short hemline and very high, strappy heels. She still barely came up to his shoulder. They could chat here, he decided with another glance at the shoes.

"Something wrong?" she asked. "Too dressy?"

"No. You look great." He smiled. "I couldn't get a reservation till eight. Want to hang out here for a bit or—"

"Of course," she said graciously, stepping aside to let him in and closing the door behind him.

He made his way into a small living room. Bookshelves filled to overflowing lined the wall adjacent to the fireplace. The room was cozy. There was an overstuffed white loveseat and matching recliner, oak furniture and across the room, a wall covered in photographs. Crossing the room, he stood in front of them. Kate joined him, standing so close he could feel the heat radiating from her and smell the lightly floral scent of her skin. A surge of lust went through him. He was becoming accustomed to that reaction.

"Your mother?" he asked, softly, gesturing to a black and white photo of a woman tenderly gazing at an infant in her arms.

She nodded. "Diana took that of Mom and Emma. Lucky for us, Diana is an amazing amateur photographer."

Kate indicated the wall. "She took most of these." There were black and white photos of the two girls at various ages, graduation pictures—each matted and framed in black.

"Amazing." He spent a few more minutes examining the wall before settling himself on the loveseat.

"This place is nice."

"Thanks. When my mom was alive, we rented a three-bedroom house closer to town. After she died, we didn't need that much space. We were lucky to get this place."

"Who lives in the big house?"

"The main house?" She grinned. "No one, usually. The owner was a friend of Roy's. He bought this place for his third wife twenty years ago and she kept it after he died. She comes for a few weeks several times a year. She's French and spends most of her time over there, but likes having someone live on the estate and take care of things. We like the cheap rent."

"So you manage the property?"

"In a manner of speaking; there isn't much to it. I contact her if things need to be done. She hates to be bothered with it, so I usually try to hit up Roy for the small stuff. I deal with the landscapers, the pool company. That sort of thing."

She perched on the edge of the recliner and there was an awkward pause.

"Can I get you anything?"

"I'm good, thanks," he said and blew out a breath. Her inexperience had preoccupied him much of the day. "So, can I ask about your relationship history?"

She examined him with those enormous, unblinking, light green eyes. "If I can ask about yours."

"That's fair. I'm sure you know most of the dirt since you did a search online."

She scoffed at that. "Please. That just tells me names and dates." She took a deep breath. "It's pretty sparse. A couple of relationships that lasted several months in college, and one that lasted four months since. It's not like I don't have any sexual experience, I just never had sex."

"The four month guy?" he asked.

"A year ago I went out with a guy my friend Ava set me up with. He wasn't over his last relationship. One night we were at the movies and we ran into his ex-girlfriend. It wasn't a scene but it was clear they still had feelings for each other. I bowed out." She glanced at him, waiting.

He nodded. "That's it?"

"That's it."

"You?"

He settled into the couch and rubbed a hand over his jaw. "I didn't date much in high school—"

"But you lost your virginity, right?

"Well, yeah. Doesn't every guy?" Smiling at her, he continued, "I was passionate about music, not girls."

"Oh, I didn't realize you started playing in high school."

"Earlier than that. Mrs. Thatcher paid for piano lessons for a couple of her kids and me." He shook his head. "Her kids were required to try it, since she was a musician: piano, guitar, voice… mostly she played at church. None of her kids were interested at all, every last one of them preferred sports."

She nodded.

"I think that's how I became close with the family, initially. She loved my enthusiasm. Taught me piano, then guitar." He smiled at the memory. "She even taught me some voice stuff, which is extremely un-cool at twelve, but I didn't care."

Alec watched Kate play with a strand of thick red hair. She rubbed a finger across her mouth and his body reacted instantly. He shifted on the couch.

"Did you play sports?"

"I ran track, did some swimming. But mostly I just played guitar and piano. That was my passion, you know? I saved up to buy a keyboard before I saved for a car. The only relationships that counted back then were with music and the Thatchers."

"Can I get you something? I have iced tea or—"

"Nah. I'm good, thanks. So after high school, I moved to L.A. with Dave Thatcher. There were women, but I was serious about music. Some women want to sleep with guys in bands. That's how it goes. I wanted to play guitar and party. My priorities were incompatible with relationships." He put the last word in air quotes.

She laughed.

"Trust me, some of the guys in my band back then had girlfriends. They were not cool with how much we practiced, traveled, you name it." He shrugged. "I was far too single-minded to get serious about anyone in particular. I've only been serious about a few women over the years."

She nodded and he continued, "There was a woman I met in recovery, it was intense but it didn't last long. There were a few relationships in college and law school."

Kate was giving him a puzzled look. "Alec, you've been married twice."

He rubbed a hand on the back of his neck. Couldn't leave those out. Much as he'd like to. He nodded. "Yeah. Poppy Thatcher and Lana Larson. You probably know my second marriage lasted about eight months."

He met her eyes. Kate nodded. "I married her in Vegas at the height of my addiction and divorced her as soon as I got sober. But Poppy…" He fell silent, remembering.

"Poppy?" she prodded.

"Yeah. Poppy." He lifted and lowered his shoulders. What a disaster.

Kate's voice was gentle. "So you grew up with Poppy?"

"Yeah. She's a sweetheart. And by then, I wanted someone in my life who was real, you know?"

Kate raised her eyebrows and shook her head, her almond-shaped green eyes intent on him.

"I was sick of the celebrity crap. The women who wanted me because of who they thought I was, not who I really am. Unfortunately, by the time I realized I wanted a real relationship,

I was already too far gone into the booze and drugs to have one. Love's no match for that. Not Poppy's and certainly not mine. I wasn't ready to fix my stuff and I did my best to drag her down right along with me. Luckily she was too grounded to get into it. But she spent two years putting up with my bullshit, trying to deal with me."

She made a sound that he interpreted as pity.

"Trust me, I don't deserve any sympathy. I cheated on her, lied to her. I cut her heart out and stomped on it. I did everything to drive her away and eventually she got some sense and left."

"I'm sorry. For both of you."

"Yeah. I'll always be ashamed of the way I treated her. She was this small town kid, young, sheltered—"

My God. Kate was the same age Poppy had been when he married her, twenty-five. They were both beautiful, innocent, small town girls. What was wrong with him? He needed therapy. He was on the verge of intimate involvement with someone too young and much more innocent. If he did get back into music, he would be making the same mistakes he'd made a dozen years ago. He would have come full circle. Would he ever learn? Were these his only choices? No strings relationships or ill-fated involvements with naïve women? What a nightmare.

Lost in thought, he knew he must be staring at her with a look bordering on horror. How had he never seen the parallels between Poppy and Kate until now?"

"Alec?" she asked, her voice registering concern.

He stood abruptly without meeting her eyes. "I've got to go."

She stood too, astonishment evident in her expression. "What?"

"I've got to go." He moved to her and kissed her on the cheek. He was out the door in the blink of an eye.

*

The next morning Alec lay in bed. He rubbed his hands across tired, burning eyes. He'd barely slept. Had he really left like that last night with no explanation? Here he'd taken two days out of his crazy schedule to see Kate and work on his music. At least half of his plan was coming to fruition.

Should he call to apologize for flipping out? She was young, sweet, and too damn innocent. The chemistry between them was undeniable, extraordinary, even. But was that enough? He was accustomed to a certain type of partner, a worldly one with few expectations and no attachments. He grimaced. Kate would want strings, exclusivity. Could he do that?

The timing sucked too. His first priority was to make some career decisions. Lately his job was a series of endless frustrations, dealing with the fall-out from the millionaire egomaniacs who were his clients. Asher was fond of saying that shrinking violets didn't make good rock gods. The people who wanted that life were almost without exception neurotic, megalomaniacal, or exhibitionists, or as Asher liked to say about himself, some spectacular combination of all three. One of the partners at the firm suggested he pick up a few movie or television clients. He shuddered. Underneath it all, wasn't he just rearranging the deck chairs? Law had served its purpose. Surely it was time to resuscitate his music career.

An apology was in order.

Finally he texted her:

Sorry for the freak out.

There was no response. Nothing for five minutes. He jumped onto a work conference call, but for the life of him could not follow the conversation. Something about a contract. Every minute he looked at his phone. Was the volume off? Did he have signal? He never acted like this—as if he were fourteen. What was it about this girl?

"Alec, are you with us?" asked one of the lawyers on the other end of the phone. It had been a half hour since he texted.

"Uh, Noah, yeah. Can you repeat that section?" Alec asked. When his phone finally buzzed, he dove for it, almost falling out of his seat.

You ok?

His thumbs moved rapidly across the phone. *Dinner tonight?*

Five second delay, then *Dinner here 7*

He typed: *Bring something?*

Just you.

His palms started to sweat.

Chapter 14

The doorbell rang minutes after seven. A roasted chicken warmed in the oven, a salad sat in the fridge, places for two were set at the tiny kitchen table by the window. Two pints of ice cream were in the freezer for dessert or for Kate to drown her sorrows if he bailed again. She hated to admit it, even to herself, but his abrupt the departure the night before was a relief. Here was the real risk. The risk to her heart. Risk she had always avoided. He had been brutally honest about his track record. He dated women like the blonde in his house that day, not women like her.

His past was a series of casual affairs and philandering, and yet, despite all that, she was half-way in love with him. This beautiful, damaged man could smash her heart to bits with little effort. But part of her needed to see him again. Needed him. Reaching down inside for courage, she took a deep breath and went to the door.

He stood there in jeans and a t-shirt, tulip bouquet in one hand, teal box from Jessica's, a local bakery, in the other. She gestured him in with a trembling hand. He was such a large presence in her tiny house. Tall and broad-shouldered, he dwarfed her little entryway. She backed up a step, overwhelmed. Her gaze searched his as he extended his offerings. She took them with a murmured thanks and went to the kitchen to put the flowers in water, dropping the bakery box on the counter.

She set the arrangement on the table and turned to him.

They watched each other silently.

Every rational thought flew out of her head. Each time she looked at his mouth, she remembered how it looked locked on her bared breast in the cab, his unique citrusy masculine scent, the feel of his silky hair in her hands.

But then yesterday he ran. Maybe he wasn't interested in being with her after all.

She could never read him and especially not now. She avoided his scrutiny, dropping gaze to his shoulders, then followed the lines of his long sleeved henley—blue, accentuating his gorgeous eyes. Her gaze dropped to where the shirt ended, at the fly of his well-worn jeans. She took in his lean hips encased in denim…*Oh. My. God.*

She raised disbelieving eyes to his hot blue ones, now drowsy with lust, mobile mouth tipped up in a sheepish smile.

"It's totally out of my control," he admitted.

She couldn't help it; she looked down again, shocked. He laughed and stepped closer.

"It happens around you all the time." His expression intent. "With little or no provocation. Sometimes when I smell you …"

The hot rush of blood swept up her neck and into her cheeks.

The hand that reached out to stroke her face shook slightly as it cupped her jaw and guided it up to him. He gave her a smile, that sexy, crooked grin, before his lips met hers and she felt that craving, the ache of arousal, now familiar. Her eyes closed, pleasure streaked through her as his lips explored her face, the sensitive areas on her neck, stroking, teasing, leaving a burning trail of sensation. Her heart, already racing, accelerated as his lips moved to the pulse in her neck.

She threaded her fingers through his thick hair and urged him back to her lips. What had been a lazy seduction caught fire as their mouths met, tongues tangling. His body, taut with tension, pressed against her, large warm hands swept downward, lingering on her hips, tugging them more tightly against him. Her hands drifted to the hard muscles in his shoulders, the ridges of his abdomen. She pulled his soft cotton shirt out of his worn jeans and paused, savoring the feel of the hot, bare skin at his waistline.

His breath hitched and her hands continued, more slowly, nervous now over his jeans, the throbbing hardness beneath the soft cotton. He sucked in a breath and pulled his hips back, giving her more room to caress him. She stroked hard, the feel of his thick swelling erection under her hands making her tremble. He groaned against her mouth, swept her up in his arms and carried her down the hall. She pulled her head away, only long enough to direct him into her bedroom. He set her on the floor next to the bed and lifted her dress. She raised her arms as he yanked it over her head, until she was only clad in panties and bra. He shrugged off his shirt, then pushed off his underwear and jeans in one swift motion.

Over six feet of aroused, hungry, naked man stood in her bedroom. His body was formidable; strong, well-defined shoulders, a tapered waist, narrow hips. She reached out to rub between his nipples and feel his chest, only slightly rough with hair. He stood unmoving while she tentatively explored him. Her hand trailed down to his hips, to the indentation where his waist met his lower abdomen. Kate ran her fingers there and he flinched and inhaled sharply. She glanced up at him and his gaze seared her. She looked to her hands, above his huge, thick jutting cock, heavy with desire, she slowly wrapped her hands around it and stroked, felt it leap and pulse. Alec let out a gasp and his entire body shuddered. This was really going to happen.

He pulled her gently toward him, correctly interpreting her concern.

"Second thoughts?" he asked gently, lips playing at her cheeks, her forehead.

"No," she got out, breathless.

He leaned back and stared at her, his eyes fierce. "You're beautiful."

She looked away, suddenly shy, overwhelmed by the feel of his naked body pressed against hers. She shivered from the heat. His hands went around her back and unclasped her bra; she shrugged it off, eager to press her aching breasts to his chest. She was barely aware of him stripping off her panties, but she did feel his hand slowly, gently, spread her legs, one finger rubbing where she was hot, slick, and aching. She moaned and clenched her thighs, trapping his marauding hand. He gentled her with a deep kiss, his other hand trailed down her back. Her thighs relaxed and his long fingers stroked, coaxed and finally, slowly he pushed one finger into her. She jerked, panted and laid her head on his chest while he worked magic with his fingers.

"Ah, God," he groaned. "You are so tight."

She held onto him for all she was worth. Every sense was completely overloaded—the feel of his smooth skin, his hard cock pressed to her belly, fingers stretched and stroking, building an insistent ache within her. She trembled, legs weak. She didn't want to come this way. Not the first time. He withdrew his hand and she yanked his hips toward her, insistent, but he turned her away from him to pull back the duvet. She climbed onto the bed and lay, naked, excited, and unbearably aroused. He reached down to his jeans on the floor and pulled out a gold foil wrapped packet. He tore it, then rolled it over himself with trembling hands, the mattress dipping as he joined her on the bed.

He opened her knees with gentle hands, and she watched him tower over her; she heard his shuddering breath. Arching her back, she closed her eyes. He knelt between her legs, his hair roughened thighs spreading her smooth pale limbs still farther apart. The tip of his arousal stroked her slick cleft, and she pushed down with her hips, desperate to pull him in. She shook in earnest now. Nervous, excited, inflamed.

He planted his forearms on the bed and slowly, slowly moved inexorably forward. Despite her arousal, she gasped and tensed at the thick, hot, almost uncomfortable intrusion. She opened her eyes, met his hot blue gaze. He froze, panting, waiting, giving her time to accustom herself to his body. She shifted, trying to ease his entry and he groaned her name. Her hands went to his hips and she held him, gazes still locked, he withdrew. With an unintelligible curse, he thrust in to the hilt. A helpless cry escaped her at the sudden discomfort and they both tensed.

He dropped his head into the curve of her neck, his body heaving and damp.

"God. Kate," he said through a groan.

Slowly, he moved, giving her time to accommodate him. He took her lips, licked inside her mouth, ate at her. The discomfort passed. She knew only the insistent throbbing ache. He stroked all the way out, then slowly back in. Her legs locked around his hips and she arched to meet his thrusts. He quickened the pace, and she clutched at him, mindless, gasping. With a sudden hard thrust he sent her over the edge and she came apart with a low scream, her legs nerveless now, quivering. His hips bucked against her. She was only vaguely aware of his big body shuddering over hers as he pumped wildly into her, then came with a long, low guttural sound.

She lay still and limp under him, his weight mostly supported on his arms. He hung his head, until his forehead touched the damp flesh over her racing heart. She smelled the musky odor of sex and man, felt the intermittent pulse of her body, closed her eyes, exhausted, sated, and buoyant.

*

Slowly, careful not to wake her, Alec moved to his side, her hips tucked against his, still inside her, unwilling to withdraw from her body. One arm pillowed her head, the other stroked her silky skin from waist to thigh absently. Despite his experience, that was unequivocally the most intense, shattering, humbling moment of his life. He'd intended to prolong her pleasure, see to her satisfaction not once, but several times. Instead, it had taken every ounce of self-control to hold off. He had come right on the heels of her orgasm, and he considered himself fortunate that she had come so quickly. He had been out of control from the onset. The hunger, the all-consuming passion, the intensity of the whole experience left him stunned. She was clueless, of course; he swallowed a groan. She probably thought sex was always like that. Oh, the irony. Being with her took everything he thought he knew about sex, and turned it on its head.

"Kate," he murmured, and as she shifted, still fast asleep, he felt a wave of tenderness toward the beautiful girl in his arms. He'd never felt anything remotely like it, nor did he have any idea what to make of it. Now, lying in her bed, with her wrapped around him, his feelings were impossible to ignore. This was different. She was different. He racked his brain, trying to remember if he'd ever felt this tender affection and wonder for another soul. It was like being stripped bare. He closed his eyes and willed it away.

Chapter 15

One week of joy. Joy interrupted by Alec's frequent trips to Los Angeles for pressing work matters, but joy nevertheless. Alec felt like a school kid experiencing his first crush. They could not keep their hands off one another. Insatiable. Insane. Yet humbling and tender. Happiness had dulled his initial fears of being so emotionally exposed to her.

"You've never asked me about my sobriety," he said. Kate was lying in his arms and they were having a lazy morning. Between his work in Los Angeles and her work/sleep schedule, it was tough to find enough time to be with her.

Kate shrugged. "It seems personal. I don't want to make you uncomfortable."

"This feels pretty personal." He trailed his fingers over her abdomen, and she shivered, pressing herself against his body.

"What? Sex? Personal? This is casual," she instructed him and pressed her lips gently to his. Her scent, the feel of her hot skin, he would never get enough of her.

Disconcerted, he pulled back to look into her face.

"Kate, seriously? You have to know that *this*," he gestured to their entwined bodies, "is not casual." He blew out a slow breath "The sex part is…" he paused, searching for the right words, "unbelievable. It's like some cosmic joke that the most intense sex of my life is with a virgin." He shook his head and captured her lips.

A long time later, she brought the conversation back to his sobriety. "So tell me."

"I don't want to, but I think you need to know. I hate that I was an idiot for so long. I hate that I have days and weeks, hell, years missing from my life. A life full of holes."

She rolled over on top of him and met his gaze. "I think you are looking at it the wrong way. You are focusing too much on the holes and not enough on what you accomplished. So tell me what made you finally quit the drinking and drugs," she insisted.

"People had been trying to get me to quit for a long time, Kate. People I cared about, people I didn't. Toward the end, I'd wake up every day so sick, in pain. I couldn't function, couldn't make music. It was hell."

She held him close. "I know something about addiction," she said calmly, "we see addicts of all shapes, sizes, and stages in the hospital. I'm not judging you. I know it's a disease and I know it's hard."

He squeezed her. Most people who thought they understood addiction didn't. Anyone who referred to addicts as "recovered" clearly didn't. Temptation waxed and waned but was always there. As a nurse, Kate probably did understand addiction better than most, but nowhere near the way someone who loved an addict in the throes of their disease did.

"I'd known plenty of people in my business, friends, acquaintances, some talented people who overdosed. I knew where I was headed, and I didn't care. It wasn't like I didn't make the connection." He ran a hand over his face. "I'd promise myself and other people I'd quit, but I used every day for years. I'd suffer through a few hours of painful sobriety, maybe most of a day occasionally, but withdrawal from the alcohol and the assortment of stuff I was on…well, it was pretty bad. Then, eleven years ago, Neal overdosed and died. I wasn't there when it happened." He stared at Kate. "I know there are all kinds of ridiculous stories and conspiracy theories about what happened to him, but that's all bullshit. He was an addict. He overdosed. End of story."

She met his eyes. He couldn't hold her gaze and covering his face with a forearm, he continued.

"Cooper was the most insanely talented person I ever met, and the most unhappy. And that's saying something in this business.

He was cruel drunk, wretched sober, and yet you could overlook his utter lack of charm because he was this exceptionally gifted musician. He could go days without sleeping, just composing. He was most of the reason we were so successful at least initially. And he hated every minute of it, the accolades, the fame, all of it." He grimaced and uncovered his eyes. "He was so disgusted with celebrity and commercial success, I had to be the front man."

"What's that mean?"

"I became the face of Bliss. I was a more visible member of the band than Neal in many ways, in the press, with public relations. People who were serious fans knew Cooper was the creative genius, but to many people, I was the face of the band."

"I thought that was because you have such a great, er….look," she said.

He frowned and rubbed his eyes with his hands. "Nah, Cooper hated it, I loved it. The money, the fame, the interviews, long discussions about the 'craft' all of it. Well, I loved it at first."

"What's not to like?" she agreed. "Whatever you want, whenever you want it. Although I think I remember reading something in college about absolute power corrupting absolutely…"

"John Acton." He sat up and pulled her into his lap.

"Hmmm?"

"That quote. 'Power corrupts and absolute power corrupts absolutely'. He also said 'Great men are nearly always bad men'. He was talking about political power and tyrants, but I found it meaningful."

"Do you want anything?" he asked, finally aware they had missed dinner. "Hungry? Thirsty?"

"No." she said, quietly. "Finish your story."

He nodded. "It was great for a few years. We had our music, more money and fame than any of us had ever dreamed of. Critical acclaim. Then the life started eating at us. All of us to some degree, but Cooper and I imploded." He stroked her shoulder absently.

"That part sounds pretty horrible," she admitted.

"I think it screws up even the most grounded people," he stated. "And yet, these days I encounter artists who have had all that and somehow they figure it out. Maybe it's the music, or the band, or some philanthropic cause, family, whatever. They stay grounded even in the throes of success and come through the other side." He shook his head, baffled. "My friend Asher is one of those people."

"Asher Lowe?"

"Yep. He's been a good friend for a long time. Asher never went over the edge. Me and Neal weren't so lucky."

"I've read a little about Neal," she replied softly and clasped his hand. She had, of course, looked up Alec and his band on the Internet after they started dating. The Internet had pages and pages on Neal. The man had a cult-like following, especially posthumously.

"His death didn't even slow me down. The week of his funeral, his widow, Alicia, and I and some other people were using, a lot."

She eyed him. Her mouth pulled down.

It took him a second to interpret the look. "Is that jealousy?"

He paused and stretched, a futile attempt to unknot the tension in his shoulders.

"It's hard for a non-addict to understand, but there was no sex. No sexual interest in anything at that point. I was too far gone. So was she. It wasn't the morality of screwing my friend's wife. We were just two sick individuals getting fucked up together. There was never anything more than that. Seriously, babe, when it gets to that point, the equipment is not fully functional. At least it wasn't in my case."

He sat up, pulling her with him. "Her family came and got her into rehab. Turns out Alicia was pregnant, pretty far along. I didn't notice, probably wouldn't have cared, the state I was in. So someone's equipment was operational; hell, I don't even know if the baby was Cooper's, given the shape he was in the months before he died. It's likely it wasn't. It sure wasn't mine."

His stomach roiled. "Alicia's family called the cops, they were freaking out about her pregnancy, the drugs. And I got busted, thrown in jail." He took a deep breath.

"They moved me from the jail to the hospital to detox. This doctor came to talk to me. He gave me the usual speech I'd heard countless times before. Thought I wasn't hurting anyone but myself. Didn't see what effect my actions had on anyone around me. I had friends who cared, sober band-mates who still wanted to make music." He inhaled.

She held him.

"So this doctor just grabs me and takes me down two floors to see the babies born to drug addicted mothers." His fists clenched. "I'd been detoxing most of a week and was antsy, but sober. Looking at those helpless babies still in the throes of what I had been through. Suffering. And the injury done to them might be irrevocable. I'd been using, sharing drugs, with someone pregnant." He shuddered.

She made a halfhearted sound of protest, clearly loathe to interrupt.

"Yes, Kate, it's a disease," he said, patiently, "but it's also a choice and those poor kids had no say. That was rock bottom for me. It made me feel ill and angry, but it also made me aware and sick about what I had let myself become for the first time.

"The rehab doctor talked to me a lot that day, and I was finally listening. He helped me get into a program and turn my life around. I realized I could either kill myself using or get a new focus in my life. He helped me understand that there were too many temptations for musicians at my level. To clean up, I needed to get out. So I went to college, then law school. And here I am. A walking cautionary tale in many respects."

"Thank you," she said softly. "I'm sorry. About all of it. I'm not judging you, Alec—"

"You should."

"I'm just glad you're sober."

They were silent for a long while. Alec wrapped her up tighter in his arms.

She leaned back. "How much do you miss the music and all of that?"

"I don't," he lied.

She cocked her head, considering him, then raised her eyebrows. "I don't believe you. I was with you in that karaoke bar."

"I don't miss the life…of course I miss performing, I miss collaborating. I've been struggling with my future for a while. I always had a great work ethic and like a lot of addicts, I suck at moderation, but I'm trying. I surf. I love this place. I'm with you."

"Someone who is the furthest thing from a workaholic." She sounded mildly chagrined.

He dragged her so she straddled him. Then he used his hands to hold her head in place and stared her down. Was she serious?

"You already get something it took me a long time to figure out. You know what is important in life. You have drive, you completed college while taking care of your sister and working. You are normal and happy. I want normal and happy! I'm an alcoholic, a workaholic…I have to constantly be on guard. I don't know what's next for me, maybe a gambling addiction?"

"Internet porn addiction?" she suggested, wickedly.

He laughed.

"Come with me to Los Angeles tomorrow. You have a few days off, and I'd love to have you there."

Chapter 16

Kate had the next four days off, plus an extra day of vacation, and Alec was driving them to Los Angeles. She stared out the passenger window, mesmerized by the brilliant blue water of the Pacific that ran next to the highway. How could she have fallen so hard so fast? Happiness bubbled up. She was giddy with it.

Alec's phone rang. He glanced at the number before connecting the call through the car stereo. His friend Dave bullied a very reluctant Alec into coming over for dinner. She hadn't thought it possible for anyone to bully Alec. When he disconnected the call, her lips were pressed together as she fought a smile. He looked over.

"What's funny?" he asked, grumpily.

"I want to meet this guy. I could use tips on handling you."

"Lucky for you then." There was a smile underlying his annoyed tone. "It's a madhouse over there. They have three very rambunctious girls. You sure you wouldn't rather go somewhere nice for your first night in town?"

She gave his arm a gentle punch. Her phone vibrated. She pulled it out of her pocket, checking the screen. A text from Billingsly:

I need to see you.

That made six this week. She deleted it immediately. What was his deal? She bit back a sigh and turned off her phone. Clearly her *ignore* policy was not working. Maybe Ava would have some insights on how to get rid of him.

Hours later, they reached the Thatcher's. It was a revelation to see him in this environment. Relaxed, happy, joking around, and playing with the girls, teasing Anna, Dave's wife. Kate could almost envision her lover as a family man. He was completely comfortable and the girls knew him well.

"Are you joining us for Thanksgiving, Kate?" Anna asked as dinner was wrapping up. Her husband shot her a look.

Kate blushed as every pair of eyes went to her. She avoided Alec's gaze. They hadn't discussed the holidays.

"My younger sister will be in town, and we do a small gathering with friends in Cielito," she replied.

Dave solicited information about her sister and family friends.

"What about your mom and dad?" one of the six-year-old twins asked. Kate was having a hard time telling them apart.

When she explained that her mother had died, there was a collective gasp from the little girls. Horrified, she turned to Anna. She shouldn't have mentioned it.

"I've explained to the girls that people die when they get very, very old and very, very sick," Anna said calmly.

The conversation moved on. Kate took Anna aside later to apologize, but the older woman laughed it off.

"Oh please. They kill every mother in the movies the kids watch. It doesn't affect them!"

But later, one of the twins, Vivian, came to her when it was time to say goodnight before bed. She hugged Kate tight against her tiny pajama clad body and whispered, "I'm sorry your mommy died."

Kate pulled her close, her throat thickened with the effort of holding back tears. After the girls had gone, she escaped into the bathroom to compose herself. When she finally came out, Alec was there, waiting. He pulled her close and gave her the comfort of his large warm body. His long, elegant fingers stroked through her hair and down her back.

"What did she say?" he whispered.

But Kate didn't trust her voice, so she shook her head and held him tighter.

Anna and Dave found them that way a few minutes later, still in the hallway.

*

When they finally arrived at his home in the hills, he rushed her through a tour of the each room and asked her to meet him on the patio when she had settled her things. He sat in the hot-tub wearing only a grin. She passed through the sliding glass door, suddenly shy. Her eyes darted around, aware of his heated gaze on her. She undressed quickly and entered the water as rapidly as she dared, gasping in shock at the heat.

"The pool guy was here today. I had him turn it on, thinking we'd be here earlier."

She shivered, nerves and anticipation ran through her. She made her way over to where he sat. He pulled her onto his lap, careful to keep her shoulders underwater, since the night was clear and cool. With little light pollution up in the hills the stars shone vividly.

"We should go to Tahiti," he suggested. "You wouldn't believe how bright the night sky is there."

"Mmmm. I'd love to go. Bora Bora?"

"That's where I went a few years ago for vacation, though I hear some of the other islands are beautiful too."

"You've been everywhere touring, haven't you?" How she envied him. She itched to travel.

"I have, but much of it I don't remember." His lips twisted. "The only reason I know I've visited some places overseas are the stamps in my passport. What a waste." They were both silent.

She could feel him press against her, but he didn't seem to be in any hurry. Were they going to have sex in the hot-tub? Her heart skipped a beat, then accelerated. She shivered again.

"Cold?"

"Nervous." And she was. Extremely.

"About being here with me? I'm a good host," he assured her.

"Wondering if it will work in the hot-tub," she replied, shyly, unable to meet his eyes.

His brow wrinkled for a moment, then cleared with a laugh. "How do I keep forgetting how innocent you are?"

He turned her to face him and pulled her knees onto either side his, then froze as his body connected to hers. He set her aside for a moment, then scooted out of the tub, reached back for the towels and a foil packet he'd had the foresight to bring.

"I've been meaning to tell you, I've been on the pill since high school." Would she have to explain about acne and heavy periods? God, she hoped not.

His hands stilled, then continued to roll the condom. "Okay."

"So is this a trust thing or a disease thing?" Her smile felt pasted on. This was the first time they were having this conversation and it was awkward. "Or maybe you'd rather not talk about this now."

He sighed and climbed back into the tub, hauling her onto his lap.

"It's a habit thing, with a little bit of my own trust issues thrown in. I'm clean because I've always used condoms. Where I grew up, a lot of girls got knocked up before high school was even over. I knew if I got some girl pregnant in high school, I'd be stuck in that town forever, so I was very careful, and old habits die hard."

She sank deeper into the water, stroking his arms, his chest, slick with water. "So you've never had sex without a condom?" She couldn't hide the skepticism in her voice. His drug and alcohol history aside, he had been with a lot of women.

"Never."

She turned herself to face him and straddled him. The water was hot, almost too hot, and she felt a rush of prickly heat. His arms went around her waist and her heartbeat accelerated. She didn't know if it was arousal or the heat from the water, but something was making her incredibly lightheaded. Her lips met his and it was as though she was starving for him.

She moaned as his tongue surged inside her mouth. She felt the throb of his arousal against her body and tried to urge him inside. He soothed her with his hands while she reached down to guide him to her, groaning in frustration when the water created too much friction and made his entry difficult. He stilled her greedy hips with his hands. His mouth went to her nipples and she arched her back. Their tips hardened from the cold night air and arousal. His hand went to the place their bodies were barely joined and rubbed her expertly. Frantically, her hips worked, desperate to bring him in, breath coming in pants. He pushed in, slowly, relentlessly, the water made the fit tighter, almost uncomfortable.

"God, Kate." His breath shuddered out. "Are you okay?"

She nodded, inhaled deeply and held his shoulders, her nails making half moon indentations as her body adjusted to his heavy invasion. His fingers hadn't stopped their relentless stroking. She felt her body tighten further, her movements desperate, she went over the edge and the unbearable pleasure of it drew a long, low cry from her bucking body. She was still spasming around him when he cursed, hands less gentle now. He pulled her hips hard into his, once, twice, then he came with a long, loud groan.

She rested against the crook of his neck, periodically shivering, though from the chilly air or residual tremors of arousal, she had no idea. Through her exhaustion, she was vaguely aware of his shaky laughter.

"Whass funny?" she slurred, nearing sleep.

"Oh, no you don't. You can't fall asleep here, Kate. Kate?"

*

She woke several hours later to exquisite pleasure. Thoughts still jumbled from sleep; it took her a few seconds to remember where she was, and a few more to realize Alec's head was between her spread legs. She tensed, hands automatically going to his hair and she pulled, hard.

"Alec!" she hissed. "Stop. What are you doing?"

He raised his head, eyes dark and thoroughly aroused, they glinted wickedly at her.

"I don't think I like that," she whispered, scandalized.

"Give me another minute," he whispered back, gently inserting a finger into her warm, slick entrance.

She let out an involuntary moan and tried to force her body to relax. It didn't take long before her hips were writhing, the touch of his expert mouth brought her to the longest, hardest, most powerful orgasm imaginable. She lay, stunned, eyes wide and disbelieving as he crawled up her body. He stretched over her, his tongue licked into her mouth. He thrust into her hard and fast with no preliminaries. She gasped in shock but her legs wrapped themselves around his rocking hips, creating a primal rhythm. She thought herself satiated, spent, after that unbelievable orgasm but within moments she felt the telltale weakness in her legs, arched her back and came long and hard, endlessly around him. She watched his face intently as he came, features rapt. Her heart expanded in awe.

Moments later, he rolled off, shoulders shaking with repressed mirth. She turned her puzzled, sleepy, still rapturous eyes on him.

"Alec?"

He pulled her into his arms, but she pulled herself up on an elbow to look into his laughing countenance.

"What's funny? That I told you I didn't like it? 'Cause that is funny, in retrospect," she admitted, smiling self-consciously.

"No, that's not it, but I think I'll remember the expression on your face afterward for the rest of my life." His lips stroked hers, gently. "What's funny is my complete lack of control. Sex is supposed to be leisurely you know, not a mad dash for the finish, and yet every time I get inside you, all my intentions of prolonging it get completely overwhelmed. That's never happened to me before, at least not since I was a teenager."

"Works for me." She shrugged. "Obviously." Her hand stroked down his chest, over his hip, eliciting a surprising response. He looked at her hand, hovering near his body, brows lifted.

"No condom," she breathed.

"Well. There's that. That could be part of the problem. Skin against skin with you was indescribable." He tugged her hand to his lips and put a hot open-mouthed kiss in the center of her palm. His expression held a tenderness that made her blush and look away.

Chapter 17

Paradise. That's what this place was. Kate floated on the raft in Alec's pool in the warm California sun. She briefly considered his offer to use one of his two vehicles to venture downtown, maybe take in a movie or window shop, but the idea of taking out his sports car or Range Rover made her nervous. It wasn't that driving a stick shift was a problem, but the sports car had funky paddle shifters and she had no earthly idea how to use them. Trailing her foot in the warm water, she stretched.

Alec wasn't around much, at least not during work hours, but they connected at night. That should be enough, right? So what if he had gotten too busy to do anything with her during the day. He was stressed about his job; that much was obvious. Tonight they were going to a party, and tomorrow he was going to take her home. If only she could shake the feeling that something was wrong. There was a distance between them here in Los Angeles that hadn't been there before, and she didn't know how to breach it. It wasn't anything she could put her finger on. Maybe she was just being paranoid because her feelings for him were so overwhelming? It was way too early to know if she was in love with him. Wasn't it?

The party was hours away. She should get out of the pool and take Zack for a run, but she was feeling too lazy.

Excited barks from the house had her paddling her raft to the steps. She hopped out and padded through the house in her bikini, expecting to see Alec home early.

In the hallway greeting Zack was someone she had only seen onstage in stadiums and in the pages of magazines. He was taller and more vibrant in real life. Slightly star-struck, she attempted nonchalance.

"Well, hello there!" he greeted heartily, his gaze appreciative as it swept slowly up and down her body. His deep drawling voice was oddly familiar. A big fan of his band Spade, she had most of their songs on her playlist.

"Asher Lowe." So here was Alec's good friend. In the flesh. It dawned on her that she was only wearing a bikini and her smile dimmed, as she became shy and self-conscious.

"And you are?"

"Kate Gibson." She reached out to shake his hand only to have her hand enveloped in both of his as he tugged her in closer.

"Actress?" He stroked one large palm over her shoulder and down her bare back, where it came to rest on the curve of her hip, his eyes glued to her breasts.

Belatedly, Kate realized that while she knew who he was, he had no idea who she was. Well, what was she to Alec, anyway? His girlfriend? A hookup? Before they came to LA, she would've said they were edging toward the former. Now? Who knew? Whatever she was, his friend was hitting on her.

She squirmed away, uncomfortable and irritated. Apparently he was a good enough friend to have a key to Alec's house, but not to know about her? She folded her arms across her chest and lifted her chin. He finally met her furious gaze and backed off, hands up.

"Alec wouldn't mind." He shrugged broad shoulders.

She recoiled. "I do," she returned coldly. *Ick.*

He laughed, not offended, and looked around idly. "Where is the man?"

"Work," she replied stiffly, maintaining her distance.

His expression registered mild surprise. "And you're here because?"

"Because he invited me." Had he even knocked? Maybe she hadn't heard it because she had been in the pool.

"Ah." He was still obviously puzzled. "From?"

"From Cielito. Not that it's any of your business." She didn't care if he was good friends with Alec. He was an irritating, lecherous jerk.

He stared down at her, frowning.

"Why don't you come back later?" She put one hand on a bathing-suit-clad hip and gestured toward the door authoritatively with the other.

He grinned at her diminutive form appreciatively. "Kicking me out? I don't think so. Got coffee?" Without waiting for an answer, he left her in the entryway, headed toward the kitchen.

Grumbling under her breath about arrogant jerks, she opened the hallway closet and rifled through jackets and coats until she found Alec's hooded sweatshirts and pulled one on. It was warm and almost reached her knees. Once covered adequately, she followed him to the kitchen and jumped up on a stool. He held out the carafe.

"No thanks."

"So, Kate Gibson from Cielito—" He stopped abruptly as her cell on the island counter both vibrated and rang simultaneously. Alec's ringtone, Asher's song.

He froze, then his eyes crinkled, amused. He winked at her and continued, "—with excellent taste in music."

She picked up the phone, swiveling the stool, turning her back on Asher. "Alec," she greeted.

"Hey darlin'."

"Are you calling to cancel our lunch?" She recognized his apologetic tone and gritted her teeth. "Alec, I'm leaving tomorrow."

"I know, I know. I'm sorry. Honest to God, work this week has sucked."

She sighed.

"I'll take you to lunch," Asher put in, his deep voice a low growl.

She shushed him.

"Who was that?" Alec's tone went from distracted to sharp and suspicious.

"Asher Lowe. He let himself in," she stage whispered and Asher laughed.

"Put him on," Alec's reply was terse and unfriendly.

She shrugged, handed Asher her phone and took the opportunity to go change. She put on underwear and a sundress, stepped into her cowboy boots, pulled her hair into a messy knot and re-applied sunscreen.

When she returned Asher was kicking back on Alec's patio under an umbrella at the glass topped table, sunglasses on, posture relaxed.

"Seems I'm taking you to lunch," he said, smiling widely. "Don't worry. I'm not going to make a pass." Her posture became less defensive. "I want to spend some time with the woman who has my buddy in a tizzy."

A startled laugh escaped her. "A tizzy? Hardly," she replied honestly. "He's been blowing me off since we arrived."

He flipped his hand. "That's Alec. Work, work, work. Consider yourself lucky if you get any time with him. I do. Besides," he looked at her from over the rims of his sunglasses, "I got the hands off lecture from Alec. First time ever. So naturally my curiosity is…aroused." The lecherous grin was back, but it seemed more like a reflex. His eyes were full of intelligence and calculation, not lust. She decided to relax. If he and Alec were friends of such long standing, he wouldn't pursue her.

"I told him I was taking you out since he was so busy." This grin was pure wickedness and hinted at some inside joke. She shrugged inwardly. It would be nice to go somewhere. He looked her up and down.

"Ready?"

"Yep."

Pulling the front door closed behind her, he locked it.

She froze on the walkway, staring at the car in the driveway. They were going to go in *that?*

"Great, isn't it?" He bobbed his head, indicating she should get in.

"What is it?" This was a car for a superhero. It was silver, low slung and sexy. Gorgeous. It also seemed more appropriate for a racetrack, not the street. She said as much and Asher bestowed a dazzling smile on her, a genuine smile, not his half-lecherous grin.

"It's a Bugatti Veyron. Wait till you get in, if you think the outside is great."

He was clearly having fun on the winding road down the mountain. Unfortunately, she couldn't seem to relax her death grip on her purse.

He reached over and patted her hand reassuringly, but slowed down.

An hour later, Asher paid the restaurant bill over her protests. From the happy, astonished expression on the waiter's face, he had left a generous tip.

By the time he got the car back from the valet after lunch at the exclusive West Hollywood restaurant, she could see why Alec liked him. He didn't take himself too seriously and was easy to talk to. He was not, however, at all subtle about trying to elicit information about her relationship with Alec. Since she didn't know the status of their relationship, he was out of luck.

"What now?" he asked.

"Alec said he'd be home around four-thirty. He wants to go to a party tonight." She checked her watch; it was after one.

"Plenty of time. What should we do?" He rubbed his hands together. "I have a free afternoon."

She shrugged. "What do you suggest?"

"Shopping?"

She shook her head. No money for that. Not with Emma's tuition sucking up the rest of the life insurance money. It was becoming more and more difficult to cover her and Emma's living expenses on her salary.

"Touristy stuff? Griffith observatory?"

"I was here during the summer with my sister. We spent the weekend doing Grumman's, Griffith Park, even Universal Studios." She smiled at the memory.

His eyes lit up. "Cirque de Soleil is in town, you ever see them?"

"No, but I've always wanted to," she replied, excited.

"I'll bet I could get us in to where they're practicing, if you want to go?"

"I'd love to!" she squealed, unable to contain her excitement as he peeled out, merging into Los Angeles traffic. She tightened her grip on her purse and closed her eyes.

*

Asher looked over at his passenger. Kate was back to her death grip on the purse. "We're here." He re-parked the car, smiling at her. She really didn't need to be nervous. He was an excellent driver. He held the door for her. Now that he'd had a chance to spend time with her, he was suitably impressed.

He'd known who she was, of course, as soon as he walked into Alec's house. He made it his business to know what was happening in the lives of the people he cared about. Asher recognized her from news about the rescue and the karaoke bar footage he had been inundated with. She was even more beautiful in person. Radiant. She was also sweet and innocent and young. Quite a departure for his most jaded, commitment-phobic friend. Things were looking up for Alec. Maybe this woman could get Alec back into music where he belonged. He grinned when he remembered her reaction to his inappropriate behavior, but it had been amusing to put her to the test.

He'd seen Cirque a number of times. Growing up in Las Vegas, there were few shows he hadn't seen. His parents divorced when he was a child, and his billionaire father had been awarded custody. His mother was a hot mess—and that was putting it euphemistically. Though she lived in Los Angeles, he avoided all contact with her. A former actress, now blackballed in Hollywood for her antics, her exploits back in the day could have given today's starlets and their scandals a run for their money.

The experience of seeing Cirque de Soleil through Kate's eyes was startling. She was awestruck. That much was obvious. He watched her wiggle to the edge of her seat when the acrobats preformed some thrilling move. She clutched his arm several times, wholly unaware she'd even done it. Her actions were child-like in a way, but there was nothing childish about her.

Asher took his time studying her. He was protective of Alec. There weren't too many people he was tight with in his industry but Alec was a good friend. He considered himself lucky to have met Sawyer when they were both getting started. Not that it wasn't a friendship with a few bumps in the road.

He was the product of two individuals with astonishing affluence and exposed to the assorted ills that accompanied fame and financial success from a young age. Raised by a largely absent billionaire father and an indifferent, narcissistic Hollywood icon mother, Asher was unexpectedly grounded. Alec and most of Reeking Bliss went off the deep end with drugs and alcohol just about the time Spade hit mega stardom. Asher had participated in an intervention or two over the years and had enough exposure to addiction in all its forms to realize better than most that he would either lose his friend to drugs and alcohol, or Alec would sober up.

Asher's vices ran to fast cars and faster women. He was jaded and bored, sure, but that came with the life. He didn't realize how jaded and bored until he spent time with someone like Kate. Though come to think of it, he didn't actually know anyone like Kate.

When the practice ended, she turned to him, beautiful green eyes shining, joy transparent on her animated face. They stood and she gave him a hug and thanked him profusely.

"That was so amazing!"

"Do you want to go backstage and meet some of the performers?" he asked.

She hung back, shyly. "Oh, no. I mean, no, really. That's okay."

"They'd be just as happy to meet me."

She burst out laughing.

He grinned back at her. "I don't just sound like an arrogant ass. I am an arrogant ass."

She nodded. "Maybe. But at least you are self-aware? And besides, I'm sure you need a very healthy ego to be a rock star."

"Now there's positive spin. I should hire you to do my promotion."

"Sounds like you handle that fine all by yourself."

He took her hand, marveling at how small it felt in his large palm and led her backstage, then excused himself to talk to security.

*

Kate watched him walk away. Moments later, Asher winked and gestured her over. He signed an autograph for the security guard. As he had predicted, the troupe were thrilled to meet Asher and she was thrilled to meet them. She met a few performers then stood back, shyly, watching him. He was polite, charming and at ease, signing autographs and posing for pictures. He joked with men and women alike. She should get a picture. Emma would love this. She rifled through her bag for her phone, twice. Three times. She stood there, stumped, frowning. Had she left it at the restaurant?

"What's up?" Asher came over, correctly interpreting stress on her face.

"My phone…"

"I may have had it last, remember? I put it back on the kitchen island."

She stared at him. "I *forgot* it?" Being available for her sister and occasionally for work was paramount. She had quite literally never left the thing behind.

"What time is it?" she asked, unaccountably panicked.

"After four."

After four? Her heart raced. "Oh, my gosh! I need to get back." She wasn't sure what she was more stressed about, the idea that her sister couldn't reach her in an emergency or the fact that she'd been incommunicado from Alec most of the day.

Asher tried Alec's phone. No answer.

"C'mon. I'll take you home."

They were stuck in LA rush hour for over an hour, so she used Asher's phone to call her voicemail. Four messages. All from Alec. Each message progressively more irritated, anxious and impatient until the last, when his mood devolved into angry. He'd cursed, barked, "Call me back," and hung up.

She disconnected the phone, eyes wide and handed it back to Asher.

Asher glanced over and grimaced. "He pissed?"

She nodded and stared at him, baffled. "He left four messages. The last message was…" her voice trailed off. "He was mad," she breathed. *So mad.*

She glanced at Asher. He didn't look surprised.

"What is his deal?" She half turned in her seat and finally the sheepish expression on Asher's face registered. Guilt.

"Oh, Asher. What did you do?"

He downshifted on the hill, the motor revved.

She rubbed her temples, biting her lip. He glanced over at her, and cursed under his breath. "Don't worry about it. I'll fix it."

She was silent for the rest of the ride.

*

Alec sat fuming on the living room couch. He'd told Asher to leave Kate the fuck alone. Did he? Of course not. Instead, he'd taken her out and texted *Girlfriend is fucking hot* and sent him a picture of her, looking radiant. Kate had left her phone. Left her damn phone. She *always* kept it on her. She was probably enthralled by the great Asher Lowe. Alec threw a cushion across the room. He'd been a jackass the last few days, prioritizing work, but he hadn't expected *this*.

The growl of the Bugatti pulled him from his thoughts. He sat, hands clenched and made an effort to reign in his temper. He heard them enter, quietly, cautiously. He watched Asher's charming smile die a quick death at his expression. Kate was white with anxiety and something else. Guilt? He interpreted it as guilt immediately and his gut clenched.

"I'm sorry, Alec. I left my phone," she said quietly, from across the room.

Alec barely spared her a glance. She looked between the two men, staring at each other.

"Alec?"

He finally looked at her and she halted on her way across the room to greet him. He forced an even tone he didn't feel. "Why don't you get changed? We should leave in an hour."

He turned his attention back to Asher.

Kate mumbled something and left the room. He watched her grab her cell phone from the kitchen on her way to the master bedroom.

Asher rubbed his hands together, and put them up. "Nothing happened, man."

"I know that." Alec threw himself down onto the couch, scowling. Was this jealousy? The thought made him bolt upright.

"I shouldn't have fucked with you, but I was curious." Asher answered the glare with a lazy smile. "And boy, did my curiosity get satisfied."

Alec half rose out of his chair at the innuendo.

Asher laughed, clearly torn between amusement and astonishment. "Do you think that I would do that to you? Who is it you don't trust? If I wasn't so amused, I'd be damned insulted. My friend, you have something here, try not to screw it up."

Alec grunted.

"I'm in town all week," Asher said and rose from the couch. "You promised we'd get together."

Alec walked him to the door. "I'm taking her back to Cielito tomorrow, but I'll be in LA most of the week."

"Good." Before he closed the door, he heard Asher whistling as he climbed into his sports car.

Chapter 18

Kate's guilt over forgetting her phone was rapidly giving way to anger as she changed clothes. Alec was too busy to take her to lunch, pawned her off on his friend, and was furious when she returned because she forgot her phone? It didn't make sense. Her heart had been walled off for so long, she didn't know what to do with all the emotions rioting through her. Anger, fear, disappointment. Like it or not, he had crashed through the barriers she'd erected around her heart. Perhaps it was time to cut her losses and protect herself before this got altogether too painful.

Twenty minutes later, Alec helped her into the car. He started the vehicle and turned toward her.

"Sorry, Kate."

She grunted, refusing to meet his eyes, playing with the hem of her dress. He reached out a finger and tilted her chin until she met his gaze. She raised her eyebrows. Waiting.

There was real remorse there and he looked pained. "I'm sorry. I was worried, then I got mad."

"Okay."

He grinned and she returned his smile.

"So what kind of party is this?" she asked.

"Eh, television and movie people mainly. There's a guy I need to talk to. We don't have to stay long."

"Good."

Once they arrived at the party in the Hollywood hills, Alec greeted a few people. Only a modicum of his usual charm was evident, and she noticed the smile he directed at her didn't reach his eyes. Tension strung her taut. She didn't know a soul.

"You can go mingle if you want," she offered.

"I'll see if I can catch the guy I'm supposed to meet." He kissed her cheek, absently, and left.

Well. This was awkward. She recognized a few actors but would never in a million years go chat with them.

She smiled to herself. If only Emma were here. She'd be dragging Kate to meet celebrities right and left.

She turned as an older man approached her. He was short, oddly muscular and wearing clothes that would be more appropriate on a much younger person.

"How you doing?" he asked, his words inflected with a thick, New York accent.

"Good." She gave him an absentminded smile.

"Whatcha here for?" he asked bluntly as his gaze drifted from the top of her head where her hair was piled up, to the tips of her slingback clad feet, where cherry red toes peeked out.

"I'm here with a friend," she responded, amused by the once-over from a man nearly old enough to be her grandfather.

"Bullshit," he replied, smiling.

She gave him her full attention with a frown. "I'm sorry?"

"What project are you looking at?"

"I don't understand."

"You're an actress?"

She smiled at the misunderstanding. "No."

"Well, you're too short to be a model."

"True," she agreed, still smiling. What a strange, blunt man.

"With an overbite."

Her smile vanished. How rude.

"What are you looking for?" he asked, impatiently.

She looked him straight in the eye. "Mr… ?"

"Butler."

"Look Mr. Butler. I don't know what you're driving at. I'm here with a friend. I don't have a project. I'm not an actress. I'm not in the movie business." She wanted to finish with "now go away!" but wasn't sure his attitude warranted that level of rudeness.

He gave a short bark of laughter "Movie business. I like that. Do you know who I am?"

"I have no idea." She smiled, showing all her teeth. "Care to enlighten me?"

"Aren't you here with Alec Sawyer?"

She nodded.

"And you're not in the business?" His eyes were shrewd.

"Nope."

"So what do you do?"

"I'm a nurse."

"Ah." He brightened and snapped his fingers. "Yes. Alec's nurse."

She rolled her eyes but felt heat creep up her neck. Good Lord. *That's* what she was?

"You and Alec saved someone." He tapped his chin. "From a car wreck?"

Kate started to interrupt, but he shushed her, "I'll get it, give me a minute. Right! The surfer. Yes."

She nodded, eyes darting around the party, her smile forced. Where was Alec?

"Good for you, but especially good for Alec, that kind of press. He's done a remarkable job remaking his image. Did he bring you here to introduce you to some people, for your story? Maybe a television movie or something?"

Her eyes widened as she realized what he was getting at. She laughed. "No, no. Not interested."

He froze, drink midway to his lips. "You are stunning when you laugh."

"Thanks," she said, drily.

"I could use you in something. Give me a minute." He steepled his hands over his mouth and frowned at her.

Kate flushed, unaccustomed to being scrutinized solely based on her looks. Who the hell was this guy? With her luck, he was probably a porn director. Swallowing a giggle, she glanced around. Where was Alec?

He smiled. "I know just the thing. Give me a headshot before you leave town."

Kate shook her head. "I don't know who you are or what your business is, but I'm not interested in a job. I have one I'm happy with. I'm just here with Alec."

"Then sweetheart, why are you at this party? This party, hell, this town, is all about networking. Alec Sawyer doesn't bring sweet, young things to these kinds of shin digs. He brings barracudas looking to get a leg up." He didn't seem unkind, only puzzled.

"Well, maybe he's trying to network."

He raised an eyebrow.

"Okay, well…" She looked around, eager to extricate herself from this odd conversation.

The expression on her face must have given her away for he gave a shout of laughter. "Honey, I can't remember the last time someone wanted me to get lost. See those people eyeing you?"

She looked around. There were, in fact, a number of people, casually standing on their periphery, looking at them.

"They're all waiting to talk to me about some new screenplay or actress or director or whatever."

"Oh. I've taken up too much of your time." She inched away.

He stepped toward her, smiling broadly.

"Trust me, this is a unique experience. Let's see if I know how to talk about anything other than the industry. Hmm." He brightened. "My sister is a nurse, back on Long Island where we grew up."

"Cool. Where does she work?"

"Hospice. But she's mostly retired."

"Oh, hospice is wonderful. Our local hospice took care of my mom at the end of her life."

"Mine too. Sorry for your loss."

"Sorry for yours. How did your mom die?"

"Lou Gehrig's a long time ago."

"I'm sorry. That's really sad. Tough way to go."

"Yeah." There was a world of pain in that one word. "Yours?"

"Breast cancer. She was sick for about three years. I think she only hung in there to see me turn eighteen so I could take care of my younger sister."

"I think mine hung in there to see if I would ever leave her basement."

They shared a laugh.

"You're a long way from a basement on Long Island. I'm sure she'd be proud."

"Thanks." He took a healthy swallow of his drink. "I got my big break right before she died. Bad timing. I'd been writing all my life, finally hit the jackpot with a screenplay, moved to LA, started taking meetings, stars were signing on. My project was moving forward and I didn't give a damn."

She reached over and squeezed his hand. They shared a look of understanding.

Alec appeared at her side. His face was a rigid, hostile mask.

She blanched and her stomach turned over.

"Nice to meet you, Mr. Butler."

"You too." Butler fished around in his pocket and handed her a business card. "Send me a headshot." Kate mustered a smile and shook her head, then tossed the card in her bag. Alec hand closed around her upper arm, almost painfully tight.

Butler raised his glass to her.

Alec pulled her none too gently out of the room.

His eyes flashed. "Looking for a new job?"

She stopped and yanked her arm. "Don't be ridiculous."

"Sorry. I just don't like to see the woman I'm with cozying up to the likes of him—"

"What the hell, Alec? He was kind—"

He scowled. "He's a shark and eats women like you for breakfast."

Kate glared. "Are you jealous?"

He snorted.

Her heart seized up.

"Why are you behaving this way, hot and cold? I'm getting whiplash trying to keep up with your mood swings."

"How about I give you hot then?" he growled, dragging her with him. Alec strode down the hall, Kate in his wake. He tried several doors before finding an empty office, pushed her into it and locked the door behind him.

He reached for her and she put both her hands on his chest. "Alec."

"I want you." His hands behind her back, tugged her toward him.

She leaned back. "Too bad. You are totally freaking me out—"

"Then we're even."

Kate stared at him, open-mouthed. What was that supposed to mean? He took advantage of her distraction, pulling her to him. Kate lost her balance and dropped her purse. Alec put one arm under her hips and the other behind her head. He brought her to his eye level and lowered his mouth to her neck. It was electrifying. Backing her up, until she hit the door, he held her against it with his body. He smelled of sea and citrus and something else that she had come to recognize as pure, masculine Alec. His body was hot and hard against hers. Her stomach clenched and she felt the overwhelming ache of arousal that only he triggered.

Her lips met his again and again; she wrapped her legs around his hips.

Without preliminaries he thrust his tongue into her mouth, ravaged her, and she gasped. This was no tentative, exploratory kiss. It was hot and hard and desperate and given her current state, racked by stress and adrenaline, she was immediately as out of control as he was. She urged him on, running her hands through his thick, soft hair. His mouth caught her moans, her dress hiked up until all that separated her from him were her sheer panties and his pants. She rubbed herself against him, her mouth glued to his. Their tongues mated ardently, they fed at each other.

She could feel his huge erection straining against her. His free hand went under her dress to her breast, popping it free of the confining fabric of her bra. His mouth left hers. He held the tip to his lips, sucking the peak into his mouth so hard it was almost painful. She moaned and locked his head to her with her arm. His hands went to her hips to grind her harder against the hot strength of his arousal, his mouth still torturing her nipple. She felt her legs start to go boneless and had a split second to realize that she was about to come, hard. Frantic, she tried to raise her hips, but his hands were locked on them, stroking her against him. Desperate, she pushed against his head, his shoulders. It was too late. She stiffened, her back arched and she came with a long, hoarse cry that broke the silence in the room. She sank against him panting.

Awareness came and with it the hot flush of mortification.

His body was immobile, but she could still feel him pressed against her, still fully aroused. She covered her flushed face with a shaking hand and tried to unwind her legs.

He stopped her, pushing her harder against the door. Tremors wracked his body. He put one hand between them and fumbled with the zipper of his pants.

She looked down, eyes widening as she watched his hands pull his erection out of his pants. He reached beneath her dress and pushed aside her panties. He raised his head and she gasped at the look in his intense heated gaze, his flushed face deadly serious.

"God. Kate."

Her mouth went dry.

He growled low in his throat and pulled her hard into him, thick and hot against her. The turgid flesh pressed at her slick entrance. He held himself up and pushed into her, slowly stretching her, blue eyes meeting and holding her slumberous green gaze. Resistance made her moan low in her throat at the discomfort, but he worked himself deeper and deeper into her, until he was fully seated.

They were both panting, eyes locked, staring. It was shockingly intimate, that familiar almost uncomfortable fullness, and it triggered weakness in her legs.

Oh no. Not again.

Something must have registered in her face, because he angled his hips, withdrew and ground against her forcefully. She came apart instantly. Before she came all the way down, he was pounding into her so aggressively it would have been painful had she not been so aroused.

She felt him tense and pause on a thrust that seated him all way inside her. He came with a long, agonized groan.

Against a door.

In a stranger's house.

Was he insane?

Was she?

He leaned his weight away from her. She unlocked her legs from behind his back. Weak and trembling they refused to support her and she slid down the door to land in a lethargic puddle. He re-zipped his pants and stood looking at her on the floor. She waited for him to speak.

He didn't. After a moment, he gently helped her up from the floor, handed her purse to her and opened the door. He led her to a bathroom where she spent an inordinate amount of time staring into the mirror. Looking at the reflection of someone she didn't recognize. A woman who had just had wild, uninhibited, sex against a door at a party.

*

Alec learned against the wall on unsteady legs and stared at the locked bathroom door. Had he really done that? Completely lost control? He'd been out of whack emotionally since he met Kate, but that scene just now in the study—that was totally over the top. What must she be thinking? Had he hurt her? Oh God. What if he'd hurt her? Mind racing, unable to form a coherent thought, shame and self-loathing created a desperate desire to flee.

He walked into the living room and spotted a couple of people doing lines of cocaine on the far side of the room. He felt himself moving, against his volition, over to the group in the corner. There he stood, watching. *Wanting*. He knew what that would be like. How it would make him feel. He missed it. Craved it. One bump. Just one.

I need to get the fuck out of here.

On autopilot, he turned toward the front door. He bumped into a woman, clad in the green and black of the catering company.

"Hey." He stopped her. "Can you do me a favor?" He reached into his back pocket, took a handful of bills out of his wallet and stuffed them into the woman's hand. "Can you find a redhead, in a blue dress? Her name's Kate. Take her home to Cielito?"

The woman looked down at the hundreds in her hand with a grin. "Sure thing."

Without a backward glance, he continued out the front door, grabbed his keys from the valet and found his car. He drove aimlessly. Considered going back to the party. No. It wasn't safe. Hell, he wasn't safe. What had he been thinking, treating Kate like that? Jesus. She must hate him. Just like Poppy. He'd been an animal. He didn't want to see her eye with the same disappointment and mistrust Poppy had near the end of their relationship. *God.* He needed to find a meeting.

*

Bracing herself, Kate opened the door. He wasn't there. Making her way down the hall on shaky legs, she cursed her heels. Wow. That had been something else entirely. Had Alec been handling her with kid gloves this whole time? She bit her lip. Admittedly, sex against the door in the study freaked her out a bit. They had never gone at each other like that. It was exciting and a little scary. She frowned. Where the hell was he?

She came to a halt in the threshold of the door to the back patio where most of the guests were gathered. Kate searched the backyard. Not there. She entered the house again. There were several shut doors throughout the house, but she was afraid to open them. She had seen people doing drugs in the living room. Would there be people in the bedrooms? Doing what she and Alec had just done? She didn't want to walk in on that either. Her stomach was balled into a hard little knot. She pressed her fist against it. He couldn't have left her here. Could he?

What the hell? She'd been searching for him more than thirty minutes. On her third pass through the house, it finally sunk in. He was gone. Kate's breath shuddered out of her throat; a wave of disbelief shook her, pushed her over into a pool of pain. She drew one breath, then another. Turning on her heel, she headed back inside only to be stopped by a tall brunette in a catering uniform.

"Kate?"

"Yeah?"

"You need a ride?"

"Uh …"

"I'm Angie. A guy gave me a grand to take you to Cielito. My car's out back."

Kate's mouth dropped open. She closed it with a snap and a glare. "Where is he?"

The woman gave her a sympathetic look. "He was headed out the front door, last time I saw him."

He left? Numb, Kate buckled herself into Angie's Mini with shaking hands. Angie kept up a steady stream of conversation. Something about how many A-lister's she'd had in her car and how common it was to take their inebriated butts home at the end of these kinds of parties. Kate only half listened.

What the hell was *wrong* with him? She checked her phone again. Nothing.

This was the second time he had bailed on her with no explanation. At least when he did it before, she'd been at her house. Leaving her at this party, where she didn't know a soul? Paying someone to drive her home?

She tuned in as Angie waved a piece of paper at her.

"I'm sorry, I wasn't paying attention. What's that?" Kate asked.

"It's a map to the stars homes. Would you believe I've actually had to use it a time or two?"

Kate cocked her head. She was not following this conversation.

"I mean, sometimes they are too drunk or stoned to direct me home. It's crazy. You know what else is crazy? How much these people spend on food when no one in this town will eat a damn thing. No wonder they get so drunk. They don't eat!"

The shock was wearing off, and Kate turned to look out the window. Her sniffing must've given her away.

Angie moved her hand from the gearshift and gave Kate's arm a squeeze. "If it's any consolation, the guy who gave me the money looked pretty wrecked too. You guys have a fight or something?"

What was his problem? The disappointment and overwhelming sadness didn't leave room for anger. Angie switched on the radio. A Bliss retrospective. Figures.

Kate spent most of the journey silently crying. How could he have just left her there? And after what happened?

Angie pulled into the circular driveway. Puffy-eyed, exhausted and heartsick, Kate opened the car door.

"Thanks, Angie."

"Good luck, hon." Kate shut the door and the car pulled away. Clenching her teeth against a new onslaught of weeping, she let herself into her house, closed the door and slid the bolt home.

Chapter 19

Alec leaned back in the patio chair, shifting his position, scowling. Damned uncomfortable chairs. He hadn't wanted to come here today. He hadn't wanted to do anything this week but hole up in his house in Los Angles and think about what a fuck-up he was. He'd finally sent the box of Kate's things with a letter.

"You're particularly morose today," Dave observed, adjusting his own position in the vinyl pool chair, while keeping a close eye on his three kids swimming in the pool. The older two swam like seals but three year old Sophy, required a careful eye. After an hour of horseplay in the pool with the kids, they sat drinking iced-tea and dripping in their swim trunks.

"These chairs suck," Alec said. "Seriously, man. Buy yourself some decent pool furniture or I will."

Dave raised his brows. "Dude. Don't change the subject. And don't irritate me. What's the matter with you?"

Alec's mouth twisted. He should have known better than to come here in this miserable mood.

"I thought Kate was—"

"It's over."

"Over?" Dave sat up and blinked at him. He settled back, eyes on the pool. "Ah."

"Don't 'Ah' me. You don't know anything about it."

Dave's lips thinned. "Don't I, though."

"What's that supposed to mean?"

Dave leaned forward resting his arms on his thighs, expression hard. "Why do you have to screw up every good thing in your life?"

Alec stiffened and absorbed the blow.

Turning his watchful gaze to the pool, Dave was probably waiting to see if the escalating argument between the five-year-old twin girls would require his intervention. "That woman was good for you."

"You met her once."

"Yeah. You think I don't know a real person when I meet one? Give me a break. I may live in Los Angeles, but I'm from the Midwest, same as you."

Alec argued, taken aback. "You don't meet the women I date."

"I rest my case."

Alec glared. "Hold on. You don't know them."

"I'm sure there's a reason for that, just as I'm sure the one you finally did introduce to us was a keeper."

"So?"

"So. You finally date a real, down to earth woman of character. A woman with no connections to the industry. A woman with a real job. A woman who is not a narcissist. A woman who wasn't dating you to further career goals. A woman who's *brave*, for chrissakes."

Alec grimaced. She was brave. A vision of her charging, fully clothed, into the water at Mar Vista came, unbidden.

"Well, you're wrong on at least one count. She may have been dating me to further her career. I caught her chatting up a producer; she got his card and everything."

Dave stared at him. "Bullshit."

Alec shrugged. Even he didn't believe Kate had been using him to get into acting. Kate who had fought to stay out of the limelight in New York.

"Alec, the woman took care of her dying mom, raised her sister, put herself through college, rescued a stranger. That takes some serious fortitude. That's a person capable of love. I'm sure that scared the hell out of you. Being with her put you in the deep end for once, and from what I saw here, you were up to your neck in it. You'll use any excuse to avoid really caring for someone. Why'd you bring her to a party with producers, anyway?"

Alec clenched his jaw.

Dave raised his brows. "Ah. A test."

Alec scowled.

"Daddy!" Both men watched Sophy as she maneuvered her way around her sisters' battle over an inflatable raft.

"Don't let go," Dave admonished Sophy who was making her way into the deep end. "Jesus, Alec, don't you think you deserve to be happy? All this self-flagellation."

Alec shifted in his seat. Damn these chairs and damn Dave for knowing him so well. "I don't know what you're talking about. I really don't. My life is great."

Dave laughed. "No. It isn't. *My* life is great. I'm not rich. I'm not that successful, but I'm doing what I want, I have a terrific, supportive wife and three awesome kids. Trust me, man. Your life is not great."

He rubbed his forehead. "It is."

"Don't bullshit me. I've known you since we were kids. My parents just about raised you. You are an incredibly gifted musician. You pissed that away. Then you pulled yourself out of a cesspool, which is something I admire tremendously, but instead of going back to the thing you love—"

"You know when I first got sober it never would have taken if I'd gotten back into music right away." Alec raked a hand through his hair.

Dave nodded. "So college made sense, but law?" He gave a short laugh. "That's a profession that attracts workaholics like bees to honey. You have nearly ten years of sobriety. Don't you think you could go back to what you love and stop screwing around, making all of us miserable?"

His response was so quiet it was almost inaudible. "I don't know."

Dave acknowledged this with a long look over his sunglasses.

"So, what'd you do to drive this girl away? I'm sure it was effective," Dave said.

His stomach dropped along with his jaw. "Is that a reference to how awful I was to Poppy?"

Dave sighed. "I wasn't talking about Poppy. You're the only one still hung up on that. We all forgave you. Poppy was the first person to forgive you, and let's be real, she came through with nothing more than a bruised heart, quickly mended, and a lot of cash." He let out a bark of laughter at the shocked expression on Alec's face. "What you settled on her allows her to stay at home with her kids, paid for their house, and provides their retirement. Time to let yourself off the hook, man."

Squeals filled the air as the older girls attacked each other with pool noodles, raft forgotten.

"Be careful with your sister," Dave commanded before turning back to Alec. "You weren't a good match, and you were pretty far gone by then anyway. I tried to talk her out of trying to rescue you, since I hadn't had any luck in the saving Alec department. I get why you married her, who wouldn't love Poppy? My sister is a marshmallow."

Alec put his head in his hands. Dave saw right through him and always had. Still, it was good to hear this about Poppy. Blackouts and guilt colored so much of his perception of the relationship with her, he didn't know what was real.

"She would be the first to admit she couldn't handle that life or you. She's happy now, and she would never begrudge you the same."

"What's wrong with me that I only want to get serious with small-town innocents?"

Dave's mouth dropped open. "Are you seriously comparing Poppy to Kate?"

"Well, yeah."

"Alec. Can you see Poppy dragging some guy off the ocean floor?"

"No."

"Would Poppy have been responsible enough at eighteen to take care of an eleven-year-old?"

"I guess not."

"I'm her brother, man, the answer is no."

"Okay. No."

"So other than age and size of the town they grew up in, do you see any similarities? 'Cause I gotta tell you man, the woman I met at my house is nothing like my sister, much as I love her."

"I guess."

"Dude. Your mind is playing tricks on you. You are so desperate for an out, any out, you're not thinking."

Stomach tied in knots, Alec stood up and paced the pool deck in front of Dave's chair. "You don't know what happened at the party." Alec threw himself back into the chair. "I lost it with her."

Dave took a sip of iced tea. "What does that mean?"

"I lost control. Sexually. With her at the party." Alec turned away. Afraid of what he'd see in his friend's eyes.

"Still not getting it."

Alec looked up and scowled.

"Well I know you, Alec. You didn't hurt her."

"Jesus, Dave, she was a fucking virgin when we met and I treated her like a, like a …"

"Sounds like you got carried away in the moment. As long as she did too." He shrugged.

Alec stared at him, open-mouthed. "I don't think you get what I'm telling you, man. *I was out of my mind.*"

"Did she tell you to stop?"

"No."

"So?"

"So, I don't *get* out of control. Not like that. Not anymore."

Dave's eyes widened. His mouth opened and he laughed. And laughed. Huge, belly laughs until he was gasping for air. When he could finally catch his breath, he said, "Oh, Alec. You poor, dumb son-of-a-bitch. Of course you got out of control. We all do when we care about someone."

"You weren't there. You don't know," he insisted, stubbornly.

"I'm confused. Was she mad at you, after?"

Alec looked away again. "No…I mean…I don't know. I had to leave."

Dave's mouth fell open. "You left her at the party? Two hours from home?"

Alec rubbed his face with his hands. "I paid someone to take her home."

Dave let out a low whistle. "*Jesus*, Alec."

"I know. *I know*."

"She must be pissed."

"I sent her a letter."

Dave shook his head. "A letter? You sent her a *letter*? Oh, Alec, Alec, Alec. You have seriously fucked this up."

"Daddy! Come play with us."

He stood, staring down at Alec. "My advice? Fix it, if you can."

Dave walked to the edge and cannon balled into the pool. Alec put his head in his shaking hands. He needed to do more than hit a few meetings. He needed to talk to his sponsor.

Chapter 20

Work was interminable tonight and it wasn't even half over. To make matters worse, a box of the things she'd left at Alec's house in Los Angeles earlier in the week had shown up at her house yesterday. Along with a letter. A letter apologizing for his behavior at the party. For "crossing boundaries, losing control, hurting her and abandoning her." He hoped she could eventually forgive him. It was clearly heartfelt; it was just as clearly an end to the relationship.

She told herself she was through crying, but that didn't seem to stop the tears from flowing. Kate hurried down to the storage area to get more linens. She turned with an armful of sheets, blankets, and towels and froze.

Blocking her exit, was Billingsly. He looked thinner. Paler. Must be all the surgeries he was doing taking their toll.

Kate glanced heavenward.

I so do not need this now.

"Dr. Billingsly. If you would excuse me, these supplies are urgently needed back on the floor." Yeah. Right. She looked at the linens in her arms. Urgent.

He moved forward. She took a step back, farther into the closet.

"Uh, what are you doing?" She strove to keep her tone conversational.

"I've been trying to talk to you, Kate. I've texted and called."

"About that. You need to stop. I'm flattered, but I'm not interested. I've made that clear."

He continued as if she hadn't spoken. "I didn't like reading about you in the tabloids. Your exploits with Alec Sawyer and Asher Lowe. Not appropriate, Kate. Not while you're with me."

With him? "We went out one time."

"And you told me you weren't comfortable having a relationship with me while you worked here."

"Yes," she admitted. "But—"

"So quit."

She almost laughed out loud, until she saw the expression on his face. He was deadly serious.

"I can't quit. I need this job. Besides, that's not even the point—"

"I can get you fired so you can collect unemployment while you find something else."

"*No.* Don't do that, Dr. Billingsly. It isn't that we work at the same hospital. Uh. I'm dating someone else."

He sneered. "Kate, I haven't seen either of them around lately. You're no longer the rock musician flavor-of-the-month. You owe me a second chance."

Her eyes widened and she leaned back, not sure what to address first. "Owe you what? We had one dinner."

"We had two dinners. I want another chance. You must give me that."

"Look, Doctor, I don't even need to give you a reason. I don't want to go out with you. Period."

Billingsly stepped closer. "I've been patient, Kate," he said softly, almost kindly, though the look in his eyes was anything but. "Enough is enough."

Is he insane?

Suppressing an inappropriate bubble of nervous laughter, she turned, sighing heavily as she dumped the linens on the cart. When she spun around, he was inches away.

"Hey." Putting up her arms defensively, she looked into his face, shocked to see it white with fury.

"I've been patient." He pulled her to him, despite her resistance. For a skinny guy he was surprisingly strong.

"Hey! Stop—"

He grabbed her ponytail and yanked her head back, she yelped in pain and he took the opportunity to grind his mouth down on hers. She could feel his arousal through the thin scrubs and a wave of panic and nausea rolled through her. She shoved at his hips, totally disgusted. She tried to turn her head, revolted by his tongue stabbing into her mouth. She bit down and he reared back, crying out in pain.

"Stop!" She screamed the word, fury pumping through her. She scrubbed her hand across her mouth, trying desperately not to retch. She wanted to kill him. She looked around for something to grab, anything.

"Kate." He reached out a hand, his eyes pleading with her.

She opened her mouth to put him down, but he took a step forward. She screamed.

A medical technician and a nursing assistant burst into the storage room. Kate scooted around them.

"Leave me alone," she spat at him over her shoulder.

With a brief thanks to her two rescuers, she headed back to her floor.

Human resources, as soon as she was off.

In the morning she stayed after her shift ended to make a complaint. Kate was ushered in after cooling her heels for over an hour in the reception area. The human resources supervisor, Marla Simpson, instructed her to take a seat.

"Kate Gibson." She introduced herself.

"I know who you are," the gray haired woman responded. "What seems to be the problem, Ms. Gibson?"

"It's Dr. Billingsly."

The woman's eyes frosted over, her expression blank.

"He won't take no for an answer. Tonight, he assaulted me in the storage area."

Ms. Simpson heaved a sigh. "You have to understand, Ms. Gibson, your credibility—"

"*My* credibility?"

"Dr. Billingsly has already registered a complaint about your unprofessional behavior."

Kate felt her blood pressure rise and she half rose out of her chair. "My *what?*"

The woman grimaced, her expression that of someone who smelled a foul odor. "We're aware you dated—"

Kate put a hand on the chair to steady herself. "Dated?"

"Dated Dr. Billingsly? We've discussed the matter with him. Although we try to stay out of these things, sometimes we're drawn in."

"I didn't date Dr. Billingsly...I went on *one* date." Kate sputtered.

Marla Simpson looked over her bifocals. "Whatever they're calling it these days, dear. I don't want to know. Unfortunately, some of the board members have seen the tabloid shots of you with assorted musicians. They're not pleased." She sighed wearily. "God knows your reputation isn't helping you, or the hospital, for that matter."

Kate sat back in her chair in astonishment. "My reputation?"

The woman put up a hand. "Cavorting with not one, but two rock stars?" She made a tsking noise, lips pursed. "*And* dating a married surgeon here at the hospital?"

Kate recoiled. Married? He'd told her he was legally separated. Had he lied about that?

Does everyone know about me and Alec? And what's this about Asher? She met the older woman's eyes evenly. "What does that have to do with anything?"

"Frankly, being tabloid fodder doesn't help your credibility. A woman of your," she looked disdainfully at Kate, "*experience* ought to be able to dissuade a man of Billingsly's ilk. Just tell him you're no longer interested."

Lips parted, Kate searched for words. She sat motionless, trying to pull her thoughts together.

"I was assaulted. At work. In the storage closet." Her anger boiled to the surface at the memory of what had happened earlier that night. And what could have happened.

"Rest assured, a report will be made." The woman looked over the top of her reading glasses at Kate. Disapproval etched into every wrinkle. "Have a good day, Ms. Gibson." She indicated the door with her free hand.

Kate rose and walked out, shaking with impotent rage. "A report will be made," she muttered to herself. She froze in the hallway as understanding set in. *A report against me.*

She saw it now. They were going to protect Billingsly and drum her out. She could try to get some kind of collaboration from the med tech and the nursing assistant, but what could they say? That they heard her scream? She stopped on the sidewalk outside the hospital. That didn't mean anything. They could probably twist that into screams of pleasure. Her shoulders slumped. She was well and truly screwed.

They'll go to any lengths to protect Billingsly.

Time to start looking for another job. Her heart sank. Despite Billingsly and management, she loved that hospital, and her co-workers. But this was one fight she couldn't win. The human resources manager had made that patently obvious. First thing tomorrow she would clean up her resume and send it out to hospitals in the surrounding area. The commute would suck, but at least she wouldn't be accosted in the supply room.

*

She'd worked two overtime shifts and it was wearing her out. Obsessing about Alec had cut into her daytime sleep. Bleary eyed, she tried recaffeinating in the break room. Thankfully she hadn't encountered Billingsly or human resources.

And Alec? What a mistake. Now she could see how her mother made such bad choices. She thought she'd known Alec. She never thought he would hurt her like this. When would this infernal, gut-wrenching pain go away?

Several hours after her shift, she ran through fog so thick she could barely see the ocean. Tomorrow night she had work.

Ava was meeting her later and Kate couldn't remember ever feeling so emotionally drained. She managed to put off Ava off for a few days while she worked, but her best friend knew how to whine and cajole and slather her with guilt until she caved and agreed to an outing.

It was far preferable to hole up eating Ben and Jerry's and work her way through all the DVR'd seasons of her favorite BBC shows than to dissect the baffling failure of her first serious relationship. Who was she kidding? Her first love. Her heart fisted in her chest.

The doorbell rang. Frowning, she pulled on her shoes. Had Ava come to get her? Odd. She'd told her friend to meet her there.

Kate opened the door and spied a floral arrangement so gargantuan she couldn't see the face of the man delivering them. He peeked around.

"Someone likes you," he drawled. "This is the nicest arrangement I've ever delivered."

"Thanks." She took the enormous vase from him and set it on the step. Glancing out at the street, across from the delivery van she saw a bright red Mercedes convertible. There was no street parking here since the driveways were big enough to park several cars. She frowned, peering at the windows and watched it roar away, tires squealing.

Was that Dr. Billingsly in the driver's seat? She stared after the car. It couldn't be.

"Miss? I need a signature." The man was holding out a clipboard and pen toward her, expectantly.

"Of course," she said, absently. "Thanks again."

Her unease dissipated as she spent a moment studying the arrangement. Three dozen pastel roses, fully opened and incredibly fragrant. Impressive. She hadn't known roses came in that many colors.

Carrying them inside, she set them on the coffee table. She pulled the small sealed envelope off of its plastic stalk and opened it. Dared she hope?

Kate, give me another chance.—B

Damn it. Not Alec then. Billingsly really was nuts if he thought flowers could make up for what he did. And *was* that him in the red Mercedes?

*

An hour later, Ava grabbed the bucket of golf balls. Picking out clubs, Kate and Ava chose positions next to each other but far enough away from the other golfers at the driving range that they couldn't be overheard.

"It was this or the batting cages." Ava smiled. "I figured you needed to knock the hell out of something."

Kate gave her a smile. "You know me too well." Her smile was belied by the vicious swing that sliced the ball down the range.

Ava took her shot with considerably less fury. "Tell me about it."

"I already told you. He's an ass. Who left me at a party where I knew no one, two hours from home. How could I be so wrong about somebody?" She swung again, a hook this time.

"So what did the letter say? Specifically."

Kate shook her head. "He apologized for what happened at the party, for hurting me, losing control, leaving me. All of it. He said everything but, 'have a nice life.'" She took a dimpled ball out of the bucket and crouched to place it on the Astroturf. Glancing up, she found Ava watching closely.

"What happened at the party?"

Kate shook her head. She wasn't ready to talk about that. To admit what happened. Even to Ava.

Ava leaned on her club. "Well, at least you finally put yourself out there."

Kate attempted a smile. "I think you mean, at least I finally put out."

"Yeah, that too. See what you've been missing?"

"It was so much more than the sex, but geez, Ava, the sex was unreal."

Ava grinned. "Sex is with a good lover is pretty awesome. And I'm sure someone with his experience—"

"Yeah, but Ava, it was beyond intense. You know what I mean?"

Ava raised her eyebrows "Kate." She blew out a breath. "The first time you have sex with someone—"

"Yes, mother? Are you about to tell me you never forget your first time? C'mon." She raised her eyes skyward. "Can you not be so condescending? You and Alec—"

Ava's brow wrinkled. "Alec is condescending about sex?"

"Not anymore." Kate said, gleefully, knocking her ball of the tee with a powerful, inaccurate swing. "He told me it was the best he ever had."

Ava coughed to cover a laugh.

Kate smiled over at her. "Yuk it up. I know what you're thinking. I would've thought the same thing. 'Oh, he probably says that to whoever he's with.' I get it. And of course it's laughable if I say it, right?"

"Well, kinda, Kate. Since you have nothing to compare it to."

"He told me it was more than great sex. He said it was a cosmic joke that the best sex he ever had was with a virgin," she said, ducking her head.

Ava froze mid-swing, put her club down and walked three feet.

"He said *what?*" Her voice raised to a shout, only a few inches from Kate's face.

Kate glanced around. "For Pete's sake, Ava." Kate backed up a step.

Ava stared at her in disbelief. "Kate, I'm ready to take back my friendship card. What the hell? He tells you that and you didn't call me? Like, immediately?"

Kate bit her cheek to keep from laughing. "I told you how great it was," she said, half-defensive, half-amused.

"Yes, well, he's very experienced. It's *supposed* to be good for *you*. I'd be more surprised if it wasn't. Dude has a major reputation with the ladies and he's been married twice; he must at least a very good understanding of the highlights of our anatomy…" she trailed off at the look on Kate's face.

"Anyway," Ava hurried on, "did he say anything besides that?"

"Just that I probably thought sex would be that good with anyone. Which I don't. I mean, you all act like I had no experience with anything. Ava, it's like the world gets blown apart and then pieced back together, and I don't usually stay conscious for the second part. I had no idea."

Ava's mouth was hanging open.

Kate giggled nervously.

Ava put her hands on her hips and shook her head. "Oh, that poor man."

"*What?* Him? He's a jerk, remember?"

"Oh, I remember. Thank you for sharing. Now everything is clear." Ava strode back over to her bucket of balls and started teeing up and firing them off in rapid succession.

It was Kate's turn to stare. "Well, it's not clear to me."

Ava replied airily, "You're no dim bulb, Kate. You figure it out." She wacked another white ball.

"You think he has feelings for me?" There it was. Out loud.

"Of course. Now, what happened at that party that you don't want to tell me?"

Kate swung hard at the ball. All power, no finesse. "The party…" She trailed off staring into space as she experienced a brief explicit flashback.

Against the door in a locked room of a stranger's house. Crazy. She shook her head to clear it.

Ava waved a hand. "Hello? Earth to Kate? I don't think I've ever seen that particular expression on your face."

A wave of heat sweep through her.

Yanking her hair out of her face, she lined up her next shot. "He might have been a little freaked out about…things. But I thought…well."

"What *things*?"

Kate glanced around, moved two steps closer to Ava and whispered, "We had sex. At the party. Against a door…and … stop *looking* at me like that."

Ava burst out laughing. "I'm shocked."

"So was I. I'm still shocked. It was crazy and aggressive and wild. And then he left." Her throat closed. Tears overflowed and, groaning, she dashed them away. "Two days later, he sent me a box of my things and that stupid letter."

Ava made a soft sound and reached out to embrace her.

"Methinks we might get banned from the driving range," Kate said thickly.

"Who cares?" Ava pulled back to look at her best friend and touch her cheek.

"It *hurts*. A lot. The heartache is…shocking."

"I know."

"I just don't understand. How could he leave me? I really wish I could hate him, but I don't. I just don't."

Ava's voice was gentle. "It sucks to get your heart broken."

Chapter 21

Kate walked out of the patient room, exhausted. She would be off for four days in—she checked the clock over the elevator bank—one hour. Approaching the nurse's station, her supervisor, Pam, looked up from her charting.

"Kate, I got a call. You need to report to human resources immediately. I've heard there have been some issues—"

"If by issues, you mean Billingsly assaulting me in the supply closet a few nights ago, then yes."

Pam stared at Kate, open-mouthed. *"What?"*

"We were low on linens last week, so I went to get some out of supply. Billingsly cornered me, held me by the hair and kissed me. I told him to stop and screamed for help. The med tech and one of the aides heard me scream and rushed into the closet." She was almost able to relay the series of events without letting fury creep into her voice. Almost.

Pam rose from her chair. "Did you make a report?"

Kate raised her brows at the older woman. "Of course I did. I was told my reputation had preceded me and I should stop dating rock stars. They're not going to oust him. He's their golden boy."

Pam collapsed into the chair, shaking her head. "Oh no, Kate, no." She slapped the desk with her palm.

"I'll say. I was actually scared of him." Kate shivered. Hadn't he said the car he was driving the night of their date was a loaner? "Do you know what he drives? I keep seeing this red Mercedes around my place."

Pam stared at her, nodding. "I've seen him in the physicians' lot. Red Mercedes convertible. Vanity plate." She snorted. "Heart fixer or fixing hearts or something silly like that."

The hair on the back of her neck stood up. "F-I-X-N-H-R-T"

"Yeah, that's it."

Kate and Pam stared at each other.

What had he said in the supply closet? That he hadn't seen her with either man in Cielito?

"Kate," Pam said. "If he's following you, that's not good. Like, *really* not good. Forget human resources, you need to go to the police. He could be dangerous."

"I'll handle it."

Pam's brows came together. "The hospital will keep him, Kate. I've been here a long time. They'll never side with a nurse over someone who brings in so much revenue for this place. It makes me furious. Furious and scared for you, Kate. I've heard things about him…mostly that he's the love 'em and leave 'em type, and a real prick in the operating room. Not this."

Kate grimaced. "It'll be interesting to see what they dredge up. I don't think they'll let me go today. They need to document a few problems with my performance to make it look legit. I'm pretty sure they'll wait until later in the week, maybe even after the holiday."

Pam's lips twisted.

Kate gave her a one-armed hug.

An hour later, the head of human resources and the nursing administrator brought her in to document work performance issues. Kate watched silently as a nurse manager she had never met carefully jotted down her statements. Had she even had contact with the patient who made the allegation? The human resources manager told her the incriminating letter had only coming to their attention this past week. Of the second issue, they didn't say much, just that a physician was not satisfied with the care she provided for his patients. Apparently, he didn't care for her 'poor attitude'.

Billingsly?

"We're investigating Ms. Gibson," the nurse manager said. "That doesn't mean—"

Mrs. Simpson, looking over her glasses, interrupted. "Be sure to sign the last document in the pile, Ms. Gibson. It doesn't mean you agree with the information, just that you've been counseled." She waved her pen. "Then you're free to go."

Minutes later, Kate sat in her car in the parking lot. Furious, but dry-eyed, she turned the car on and started home.

Running was the very last thing she wanted to do after the encounter with those women this morning, but the stress was starting to eat at her. Sighing, she pulled out her running gear. A run would burn off some of her anger and anxiety, maybe even make her tired enough to sleep.

Should she quit? Quitting felt like failure. Billingsly and the hospital were bullying her. Giving in to bullies went against the grain. Then again, most job applications had an "ever been fired or asked to leave" checkbox. She refused to spend the rest of her career being less eligible for employment.

She covered her face with her hands. She couldn't risk being fired. There was too much at stake. She was barely making ends meet now. Without a steady income, she wouldn't be able to pay Emma's bills, let alone her own.

Then there was Alec. He'd made it clear they were over. Pulling on her running shorts, she bent to tie her shoelaces. Her cell rang. Emma's ringtone.

"Emma."

The voice on the other end was dull with pain and choked with tears and barely above a whisper, but she heard her name.

"Honey, what's going on? Are you okay?" Panic and fear filled Kate.

"Kate. H…how could you?" Emma asked.

"What, honey?" She knew Emma well enough to know this degree of emotional response could be caused by anything from a break-up to a lousy grade.

"He…he didn't even know about me." The crying turned into sobbing.

A chill of foreboding swept through Kate.

"Who?" she asked, already knowing the answer.

"Dad!" she screamed. "He didn't even know about me until he saw me on television and you knew. You knew!"

"Emma. It's not…" It's not what? She wasn't prepared to have this conversation. What lies should she tell next?

"It's not what? And Mom." Kate could barely make out Emma's words through the sobs.

Kate's gut clenched.

"Mom left him off of my birth certificate?"

Kate closed her eyes and rubbed a hand over her face. "It's complicated, Em."

"You're a liar!" she shrieked. "I can't believe you kept me from my own Dad. What is wrong with you? What was wrong with our mother?"

"Emma. Calm down. It's not what it seems."

"Are you kidding me? That's all you have to say? Screw you!"

"Emma! We were trying to protect you." *What a disaster.*

"Protect me?" she screeched. "By keeping me a secret from my own father for eighteen years?"

The dam burst, Kate's control fled. "*Yes!* He's an asshole. Worse than that, he's dangerous, a criminal."

"I don't believe you. I don't believe anything you have to say. You're mean and…and…hateful. How could you, Kate? How could you and Mom do this to me?" The sobs had subsided. Her tone was coldly furious. This was an Emma she was unfamiliar with.

Kate took a deep breath. Her heart ached. "I'm sorry, Emma, I love you. I was… we were, trying to protect you from a—"

Emma interrupted coldly. "That's bullshit. You don't keep someone secret from their own father for eighteen years. That's…

that's.… I don't even know you, Kate. You're a control freak. You had to be the one in charge of the insurance money. The money, the money. I swear it's all you care about. You didn't want Dad to take care of me."

Kate's stomach lurched. "That's not true, Emma. I've tried to be frugal so you could go to whatever college you wanted. If that thieving father of ours had control, he would've run through the money years ago."

There was silence on the other end of the line. Was she getting through?

"There's a lot I need to say to you, but I hate to do it over the phone. There are documents…" she got out, haltingly. "How did he find you?"

"I found him. I hired an investigator with the money you sent for the ski trip—"

Kate grabbed the edge of the bed, legs trembling. "*Emma.*"

"I'll be home for Thanksgiving next week with Dad," Emma said, dully. "If you get the credit card statement, just…just…" Kate heard her sobbing inhalation. "It's my money, too, you know. And Dad needs our help. He borrowed the money and he's going to pay it back at Thanksgiving."

Her stomach plummeted. "You gave him money?" she breathed, horrified. "How much?"

"See? That's all you ever care about, Kate. Money. Not me, not Dad, and certainly not the truth. I'll tell you one thing. I'll never forgive you. Never." She hung up.

Kate stared at the phone in her hand. She shook her head to clear it. Dazed, she walked over to her laptop at the desk in the corner of the room.

She was barely making it these days between her living expenses and Emma's room and board and credit card charges. Now she was on the verge of getting fired and didn't have a job lined up.

Legs quaking, she sat down hard in the chair and flipped open the computer. Kate went through the log-ins on autopilot, finally bringing up the online balance for their credit card statement.

She blinked once, then twice at the screen.

Twenty-thousand dollars.

Emma had taken twenty-thousand dollars out on the credit card. She put her head in shaking hands.

There had to be a way out of this mess. Could she claim fraud? No, both her name and Emma's were on the account. She called Emma. The call went straight to voicemail. She disconnected and tapped out a text.

Please call me.

She stood and moved toward the front door. Maybe a run would provide answers.

Chapter 22

Kate was at the beach for her usual run after her shift, only nothing this morning was usual. Standing on the hard, packed sand near the edge of the ocean, she couldn't do it. Her legs refused. Run? Her legs were trembling so much they barely held her. The sun shone. The water crept up and back ceaselessly as the tide went out.

She slid to the sand, pulled her cotton clad legs into her chest and rocked. Jaw clenched, teeth gritted against the relentless pain that suffused her. And then they came, she couldn't beat the grief back any longer. Dissolving in sobs, she buried her face in her knees in a futile attempt to muffle the sound.

How had life gone to hell in such a short time? It all started here on this damn beach. And here she was helpless, alone and overwhelmed again.

Her sister was aligned with that monster who was their father. Had given him twenty thousand dollars. She should have told Emma what she knew about Matt years ago. She should have tried harder to make Emma understand about the insurance money and the cost of her tuition. Ava was right, Kate had cocooned Emma, tried to shield her.

Now look at the mess they were in.

It's all my fault.

No wonder Emma couldn't trust her. And Matt Gibson was downright dangerous.

Everything was in jeopardy now, her relationship with her sister, her job, Emma's degree, maybe even Emma. What was she supposed to do?

Hot panting breath at her ear shocked her. She yanked her head away as Zack pawed at the ball at her hip, dancing and barking, impatient and oblivious to her turmoil. She threw the ball for him, a lame effort. She was terrified she would look up and see Alec. Not now. Not when her life had fallen apart, when she had fallen apart.

Then there he was, on his knees in front of her. She raised her head and met those brilliant azure eyes. Eyes that seemed to look right through her, hard jaw perennially scruffy. Her heart leaped. Couldn't she have developed some kind of immunity to him?

Alec took one look at her tear-stained face and yanked her into his arms. He held her tight against his neoprene clad, now sandy body. The familiar feel of him, the concern so evident on his face sent her in renewed paroxysms of weeping.

Kate hadn't cried like this, ever. She cried so hard she had trouble breathing, her sobs turning into coughs amid great gasping breaths. He held her tightly and repeated her name, gently, carefully.

After a long while, she slumped against him. He gathered her into his lap. She fit her head against his chest, drained, exhausted, empty.

"God, Kate." He sounded shaken.

She made a feeble move to push away, which he immediately resisted, his grip tightening. Tears she thought were over leaked out, and she pulled away to look up into his beautiful face. He gently tucked her hair behind her ear.

"Oh, Alec. My life is…" She stopped and shivered. "Emma." Her voice broke.

"Has she been hurt?"

Kate shook her head. "She found our dad."

"Uh-oh. Come on." He stood, pulling her to her feet. "Come up to the house. Please, Kate."

She wiped at her face, unable to stop the steady stream of tears, the occasional hiccough. She nodded, not trusting her voice.

He pulled her down the beach.

"Your board?"

"I dropped it up near the house when I saw you."

He whistled for Zack and the dog came tearing toward them.

Once inside, he brought her to the master bath and turned on the shower, hot. The room filled with steam within minutes.

"Clothes off," he said. "I'll bring you a towel and robe."

She followed his directions, some part of her vaguely aware that after so many years of trying to take care of everything, someone was taking care of her. She stood under the hot spray, trying to empty her mind, but all she could think about was Emma.

Emma had paid someone to find their father.

Emma had given their dad twenty thousand dollars.

Emma hated her.

And Emma was bringing that monster *home*.

By the time Alec came back in shorts, she sat weeping on the floor of the shower. He opened the door, swore softly and turned off the shower heads. He pulled her to her feet and wrapped her in a thick bath sheet. Patiently he dried first her hair, then, impersonally, her body. Struck by a belated sense of modesty, Kate protested, grabbing for the towel. They had a brief tug of war. Alec won and finished drying her off.

She followed him out of the bathroom to the bedroom where he helped her into an old soft t-shirt lettered with the name of a vaguely familiar band. Kate watched as he pulled back the sheets on his massive bed and gestured for her to climb in. She did and he joined her, pulling her up hard against his body, his back against the headboard.

"Tell me."

She told him everything. About Emma finding Matt, the money. And finally, she told him something she had never told another soul.

In a halting narrative, eyes leaking continuous tears, she explained how her mom had finally gotten up the courage to kick

Matt out of their lives; gotten a restraining order. And, how Matt violated the restraining order and raped her mother. A rape that resulted in Emma's conception.

Kate stopped, unable to continue. Alec's body was rigid against hers. She chanced a look up into his face. His horrified expression sent her into a renewed bout of weeping. He stroked her back and tried to quiet her.

"It's going to be okay, Kate."

He kissed her forehead and continued stroking her back.

"You need to tell Emma about the abuse. Of your mother, of you. She won't be able to make a good decision regarding her relationship with her father until she knows at least some of the truth—about him and his violence. It's only fair that she know what she's dealing with. She may choose not to believe you, initially."

A moan escaped her. She pulled away to sit cross-legged in front of him, holding his hands tightly.

"But I think given your relationship, she'll come around. She probably doesn't know who to believe. I'm sure she's desperate for a relationship with her father, not surprising in light of what you've both been through. Have a little faith in her. He'll show his true colors sooner or later. You said he borrowed money?"

"Yeah. Twenty thousand. Borrowed? We'll never see it again." Kate took a deep breath. "I was trying to protect her. I should have told her when Matt contacted me. She might have believed me then. But I was so afraid—"

"Of?"

"I'm afraid she'll find out about the rape. *I* couldn't handle knowing that, there's no way she could. It would destroy her."

"She doesn't need to know about the rape." He tugged at her hair. "Something addicts learn in recovery is to make amends to people they have harmed. I'm kind of an expert in this area. When you make amends, you have to show common sense. If making amends creates further harm, skip it. The rape is a part of a bigger truth. He's abusive, has a criminal record, he's a thief and a con-man. That's the part you share. Send her the documents. But, yeah, don't let her know about the rape."

Kate took a deep shuddering breath. "Okay. I'm going to burn the police report. If anything happens to me, she won't ever have to know."

"Good. Burn it."

"What if she won't listen? Alec, she's so stubborn."

"She's going to be right here in Cielito. We'll watch out for her. You'll work on her Kate. She'll listen, eventually."

"*God*, Alec." She looked up at the ceiling, jaw clenched. "I hate like hell to lay all this on you—"

Something akin to despair flashed in his eyes. "Kate. You have to know that I want to help. You *have* to know how much I care about you."

She looked down at her fingers, plucking at the bed sheet. He put a finger under her chin and gently lifted face to meet his.

"I am so sorry I hurt you. Left you there…at that party. I'm still such a fuckup. God, I can't tell you how sorry I am." He cleared his throat.

Kate's lips twisted. "I just don't get it. Why did you leave? How could you do that…after…after."

"I was freaking out. I kept losing control. I don't lose control. Not anymore. After what happened at that party, I…didn't know what to say. I was afraid to face you."

Kate frowned, searching his penitent blue gaze. "But Alec, I was…into *that*."

He cocked his head. "You were?"

Heat crept up her neck and flooded her face. She watched her fingers play with the sheet. "For Pete's sake, Alec. Couldn't you *tell*?"

He groaned. "I thought you'd be mad. Or hate me. And as

soon as I walked back to the party, there were people in the living room…using."

"Oh, yeah, I saw them."

"I was tempted, really tempted for the first time in a long while. I was afraid I'd freaked you out with my jealousy and then what happened in that room, and, well, I ran. I ran to a meeting. Then I ran to Dave, then finally, I got some clarity talking with my sponsor. I came to Cielito to try to make amends."

"I still can't believe you left. And then there was that letter."

Alec looked at the ceiling. "I know. I'm so sorry, Kate. That whole weekend was freaking me out. I was jealous of Butler, of—."

She frowned. "You were jealous of that old man?"

He laughed, ruefully. "That old man only sleeps with twenty-somethings, Kate. But yes, I was jealous of Butler. And of Asher. Especially Asher. Jealous and angry that he got to spend the day with you. He sent me a picture of you looking—"

"He sent you a picture of me?"

"Yeah."

Kate shook her head. "I don't remember a picture."

"Did he tell you I told him to leave you alone?"

She drew back. "What?"

"I told him not to take you to lunch. I insisted on it. Typical Asher. Does what he wants, when he wants. Not that he's selfish. He's just—

"Oh, I know what he's like. I thought since you were friends, I mean, I would never—"

"No, I know. I know you wouldn't. My emotions have been … uh…extreme since I met you, Kate. The jealousy, the sex, people using drugs at that party, I wasn't thinking clearly."

Kate stiffened at his words.

"And apparently I'm not good at dealing with my feelings, particularly where you're concerned, Kate. So I behaved badly."

"And stupidly," said Kate.

"Yes, stupidly."

Kate smiled sadly at him. "I guess I can understand that."

"Will you give me another chance?"

She gnawed her lower lip, meeting his sincere blue gaze, shyly. Her heart felt like it might come out of her chest it was thundering so wildly. "Do you think you can stop bailing on me?"

"Yes." He took her hands in his and drew a deep breath. "I love you, Kate."

Her breath caught. He loved her. Joy surged through her with an intensity that left her lightheaded.

Reaching for her hand, he continued, "I know my timing sucks but—"

"I love you too, Alec. God knows I've tried not to, but—"

He pulled her into his arms, silencing her with a tender kiss. He kissed her cheeks, her brow, her lips again.

"I have so much to sort out. Work, Emma, my dad…with everything that's been happening." She looked up at him. "It's bad enough your family is awful, and that you have to deal with the messes your clients make." She took a deep hiccoughing breath. "I don't want you to deal with my messes too."

He cupped her face with his strong hands. "I want to deal with your messes. It's a privilege."

She giggled. How had this gone from the worst day of her life to the best? A pang of guilt about Emma dampened her joy.

She kissed him then and he relaxed against her. When she leaned away, he spread his hands out in front of him and shifted restlessly against the headboard, clearly uncomfortable.

"Look, I'm not a good bet. I'm an old, washed-up, twice-divorced, ex-guitarist addict who flamed out years ago. I don't know how to do normal. I really don't. I went from alcoholic to workaholic." He took a breath, watching her carefully. "I haven't had a healthy relationship with a woman, in, well, a long time. Truth be told, I'm not sure I ever have. But I'm willing to do whatever it takes to figure it out and make it good with you, and I promise not to run off again."

His jaw clenched. She could see how difficult this was for him. Her heart expanded.

"Look at you." His gaze burned into hers. "Young, innocent. God. So innocent."

"Not so much," she mumbled.

His eyebrows arched but he didn't rise to her bait.

"Young," he insisted and gave a humorless laugh. "Something I have never, ever had an issue with before."

He continued, doggedly, "You're so beautiful, it makes my insides ache, and that's not even why I'm so crazy about you—you risked your life for a complete stranger—"

Kate snorted. "So did you."

He gave her that sexy half-grin she loved so much. "Maybe I was just angling to meet you."

Sobering, he continued, "You took care of your dying mother, raised your sister, even your freaking profession is helping people."

She shook her head and let out an incredulous laugh. "It's funny how you see me, Alec. I'm nothing but a big chicken. Once we helped that surfer, I realized that at some point after I lost my mom—and finding out the truth about my dad—I stopped taking risks, emotional risks. I backed out of relationships that were getting serious." She took a deep breath. "I've been operating from a place of fear for so long." She gulped. "But... I'm not afraid to take a chance with you." Her eyes filled again.

He leaned forward to embrace her. "Kate, I'm not going to hurt you. Together, we can figure all of this out." He kissed her gently and it ended on her sob. Long shudders wracked his tall body. Lifting his head up with fingers threaded through his thick hair, she brought his mouth to hers, fiercely, deepening the kiss.

What started as loving comfort raged into an inferno as their mouths met, lips, teeth and tongues tangling. Closer, more, harder. His body, taut with tension, pressed against her. His large warm hands swept down, yanking her hips to his. He laid back, until they were reclined, side by side.

Her hands drifted down to the hard muscles in his shoulders, chest, the ridges of his abdomen, relishing the satiny feel of his hot, bare skin. Her trembling fingers unsnapped the button on his cargo shorts. The sound of the zipper the only sound in the room. He raised his hips and she shoved off shorts and black cotton boxer-briefs, pushing as far as she could, then bringing up a foot to shove them the rest of the way down. He flinched away from her knee, with a choked laugh.

Flipping her on her back, he made short work of the t-shirt. He leaned back, his eyes worshipping her body.

"Alec. Please."

With a wicked grin, he moved forward, until his mouth was on her breast. His warm, slick tongue tortured first one nipple, then the other. Her hands, tangled through his hair, held him to her for a moment then, insistently, moved his head up to hers. He groaned into her mouth as their naked, hot, flesh met from chest to thigh. *Finally*. How she had missed the feel of his body.

"God, how I love you, Kate," he muttered, staring down at her, blue eyes heavy-lidded with desire. His lips brushed her cheeks, her forehead. She groaned with impatience, bucking against him.

"I love you too, now show me." Unbearably aroused, she ached for him. Wrapping her legs around his hips, she pulled him down, bringing his hot, thick arousal against her slick, wet entrance. He shuddered, slowly working his way into her. She gasped, tensing as the pressure built, as his hot thick, flesh pushed still further, almost uncomfortably full of him.

Opening her eyes, she met his intense blue gaze. He waited, fully seated, giving her time to accustom herself to his girth. Her hips moved restlessly as her tongue licked into his mouth.

"Don't be gentle," she murmured, huskily. "Be quick."

He gave a short, pained laugh. Groaning her name, arms on either side of her he kept a slow, tortuous pace. Withdrawing, then fitting himself back inside her. She grabbed his iron hips, desperate, mindless, gasping.

"Please, Alec," she cried.

He increased the tempo, his warm damp body now held up by shaking arms. With a strangled sound, he thrust into her one final time, sending both of them sailing over the edge to fulfillment, into oblivion. He rolled off, tucking her against his still trembling body, he reached an arm down to pull the covers up. She burrowed into his warmth, and slept dreamlessly.

*

He must've dozed too, holding her in his arms. Alec slowly rose to consciousness, a niggling thought at the back of his mind. What had she said earlier? That she was operating from a place of fear? Why did that sound so familiar? Maybe because she had described what he had been doing with his emotional and professional life for the past few years. He tilted his head, staring at her.

"What?" she asked, sleepily stirring.

"You awake?"

"Barely." She yawned and stretched, drawing back so she could see his expression. "What's that look for?"

"What you said about taking risks...my music..."

"Yeah. So *do* you think playing professionally will lead you back into drugs and alcohol?"

He stared into her knowing green eyes. "I don't know."

"Well, Alec, you could just keep playing for yourself, the way you have been."

"Wait. What?" he interrupted, frowning.

She pulled up his left hand in answer. He made a fist reflexively which she gently unfurled, kissing each fingertip.

He stared at her, motionless. "You know."

"Since that day we kissed in the alley."

He jerked back to look more closely at her. "And you never said anything?"

She shook her head. "I figured you didn't want anyone to know. You sure denied it enough."

"You noticed calluses?" He couldn't believe it. Even the musicians he represented hadn't noticed.

She shrugged. "Nurses are observant about stuff like that, plus your fingertips are rough on that hand when you," she paused and her smile turned wicked, "touch me."

"But you never said anything."

"I didn't want you to have to lie."

"I wouldn't …"

"How long have you been at it?"

"I never stopped," he admitted.

Her eyes widened. "You must have written quite a lot."

He nodded.

"Years of material?"

"Almost ten years."

"Alec," she gasped.

"Songs no one has heard." He laughed. "Probably crap."

She sat up and bounced in the bed.

He laughed and sat up, guiding her into his arms. "And for the last few weeks every damn one of them a love song," he whispered.

Her arms went around his neck and held tight. She kissed him, a long, deep kiss. His hands slid up her naked back and she shuddered. It was a long while before they made it out of the bed.

*

Kate stared sadly into her lover's refrigerator. A wrinkled lemon, a jar of pickles and a bottle of ketchup were the only items.

With a sigh, she closed the door and opened the pantry. A few canned goods. Nothing appetizing. Alec had next to nothing to eat in his house and she was ravenous. The doorbell rang. Kate frowned. Should she put on clothes? This t-shirt was hardly decent. Moments later, Alec returned to the kitchen with a bag of food.

"I ordered Thai while you were showering."

She grinned. "Ah, excellent."

He dropped off the bag in the kitchen where Kate was getting out plates.

"I'll be right back," he said, disappearing down the hallway.

He returned a few minutes later holding a long, slim, blue box in one hand. Tiffany blue.

She cocked her head and frowned. "Alec—"

"I bought this in New York."

Taking it from him, she gave it a cautious shake.

"I've been meaning to give it to you. I wanted to give it to you in Los Angeles, but it was shipped here."

She took the lid off and peered inside. The tears came without warning. One moment she was smiling, the next sobbing. He picked her up from the chair and carried her and the box into the living room and sat with her on the sectional.

"I'm sorry, Kate. Is it bad timing? With everything that is going on with Emma—"

"No." She kissed him, her tears giving the kiss a salty flavor.

She pulled it out slowly by its chain, staring at the small gold, heart shaped locket in awe.

"I got the sturdiest chain, with a reinforced clasp, but all the same, I don't want you making water rescues in it. Agreed?"

Kate smiled and opened the locket. On one side there was a picture of her mother, laughing. It had been taken before her mother was diagnosed, laughing at Diana, no doubt. The other held a tiny black and white picture of Emma. Emma at five, a precocious five. Alec helped her put it on.

"Emma gave me the pictures. She mailed them a while ago. She didn't want a baby picture in there so—"

"What's this engraved on the back?" She examined the tiny script. "*Numquam perit amor*." She looked up at him. "Am I saying that right?"

He shifted beneath her, holding her gaze. "I don't know. It's Latin. It means 'love never dies.'"

She buried her face in his neck. Trying so desperately to hold back tears, her body convulsed.

"It's okay, Kate. Let it go."

When she was finally able to speak, she whispered, "Thank you, love."

*

A few hours later, Alec watched Kate eat re-heated Thai food at the kitchen table.

"So tell me more about your music plans," she insisted, forking in a mouthful of shrimp Panang.

He smiled and shrugged. "Dunno. A lot has changed in ten years. I've got people I'd like to work with. I'll see if they're available. It'll take some time."

He had to force himself to say the words. He had seen too many relationships wrecked on the rocky shores of a demanding musical career. Far too many. "There are a lot of hardships in a relationship with a working musician, Kate."

Her eyes sparkled with excitement. "The travel?"

He pressed his lips together. "Lots and lots of travel, once you're promoting something." She laughed. "Think of something else, Alec, because to someone who has never been anywhere, getting to travel is not a drawback."

"The odd hours," he said slowly. "Nights?"

This time they both laughed.

"Expensive hotels?" she asked.

"Take out or room service every day."

"Watching my boyfriend play live?" She grinned and shoveled in a mouthful of shrimp, vegetables and rice.

He frowned. "Watching women stuff their phone numbers in my pocket?"

Could she handle that aspect of the life? He had never fully experienced jealousy until that horrible day in Los Angeles. He wouldn't want to put her through that on a regular basis.

He watched her swallow and take a sip of her lemonade.

"Can you be faithful to me, Alec?" she asked, her serious green eyes searching.

"Yes." Of that he had no doubt.

Her smile was radiant. "Then I'll trust you."

*

The morning light was coming through his bedroom windows. Kate could hear the unceasing crash of the surf, surprisingly loud, strangely comforting. She turned her head on the pillow and looked directly into Alec's hot blue eyes. She stretched, caught his lascivious gaze and chuckled. "So now my problems don't seem as overwhelming as they did on the beach, but there is one other thing I need to tell you about."

She told him everything that happened with Billingsly; the weird date, his calls and texts, seeing his car on her street, the incident in the storage closet, her complaint, meetings with human resources; and finally about being written up and likely fired.

He went ballistic. She stared, open-mouthed as he leaped from the bed and prowled the room, naked and ranting. The overwhelming emotion of the previous day took its toll. She tried to suppress her snicker, but it slipped out. He paused mid-tirade, glowering at her.

"What's funny?" he snapped.

"You." She pointed at him. "Ranting and raving, stark naked I might add, about sexual harassment, stalking, and assault. Making threats to feed him his own balls." Giggles overcame her.

Eyes narrowed to slits, lips compressed into a thin line, he stared at her.

"I don't find it remotely funny."

That sent her off into fresh gales. When her laughter trailed off, he said darkly, "That son-of-a-bitch has messed with the wrong woman. Your *reputation*? *Your* reputation? I could…" He made a throttling motion with his hands, apoplectic.

"Yes, but what can we do?" she said, spreading her hands.

"You will recall that I'm a fucking lawyer," he half-shouted at her, expression incredulous.

"Well, yes, but entertainment law?" She had to press her lips together to stifle more laughter at his affronted expression.

He rubbed his hands together "Oh, I think I can handle both a stalking case and a sexual harassment case. The laws have toughened up around stalking, and I am very, very familiar with them." His tone was silky. "I'm willing to bet people will come out of the woodwork once we get the ball rolling."

"Slow down, counselor. I'd like to keep my job and not have to deal with him. It might be harder than you think. He's their golden boy, you know."

"Yeah. I've seen the billboard. What's he doing in Cielito anyway?" he asked, eyes narrowed.

"What do you mean?"

"I mean, what is a surgeon with his qualifications doing in a little town like Cielito at a community hospital?"

She cocked her head. "That's an excellent question. We're a good hospital, but his qualifications and experience are well beyond us."

"I wonder if he got into trouble somewhere."

Her mouth fell open. "He's done this before?"

"Likely, yes."

She shot straight up in the bed. "And been fired?"

He tilted his head. "Possibly, or he resigned, knowing what was coming. Stalkers are often serial offenders. He shouldn't be too hard to nail." He rubbed his hands together, clearly relishing the coming fight.

She got to her knees. "Can you find out?"

He gave her a hard kiss. It turned into a slow, sliding merging of lips and tongue. Breakfast could wait.

Chapter 23

Two days later, Kate followed Alec into the shower. One thing led to another, and they were scrambling to get dressed to make their appointment with hospital administration. He stepped out of the walk-in closet, nattily attired in a several thousand dollar conservative gray suit. Kate's jaw fell open.

Alec shot her a look. "You okay?"

She shook her head to clear it. "I'm going to miss your lawyer costume when you go back into music," she said sadly.

He grinned. "I think you'll like my rocker attire."

Kate's eyes widened. "Leather pants?" she asked, hopefully.

He burst out laughing. "You really do love the seventies, don't you?" He shook his head.

She tried Emma again. No answer. She'd emailed copies of the police reports to Emma. No response.

An hour later, with barely time for a coffee stop, Kate led Alec to the hospital administration conference room.

They were all there. The Director of Human Resources, the highest level administrators of the hospital, board members. Alec had filled her in on the basics of sexual harassment law. He'd explained that her hospital had done nearly everything wrong in dealing with her complaint.

Alec had told her that most employers, including health care systems, hospitals, and practice groups, maintained in-house procedures aimed at enforcing anti-sexual harassment policies by investigating complaints and imposing appropriate disciplinary action on violators. Most states, including California, were required to report claims of sexual harassment to the Board of Physicians. That report could result in an action on the physician's license by the Board, and ultimately suspension or revocation of the license.

Alec had Billingsly investigated. Bingo. His investigator—the best in the business, he told Kate—hit the mother lode. There was a laundry list of previous filings by nurses and other subordinates at a number of hospitals, going all the way back to his residency. The reports included invasive touching and intrusive questions about the employees' sexual practices, even stalking complaints. The hospital knew, or should have known, of his history and failed to take adequate measures to prevent future incidents. She was surprised to find that she was not even the first nurse at Cielito Community to make a complaint about Billingsly.

It was cool and fascinating to watch her lover in action as an attorney.

"Sexual harassment in the workplace is not a thing of the past. It continues to be a serious problem for working women. The way this hospital has handled complaints about a physician with a long history of sexual harassment and inappropriate relationships with subordinates is abhorrent."

She watched in awe as he took them to task.

"Let's see if what happened here constitutes sexual harassment." He held up his hand and ticked off each item as he spoke. "One: made sexual advances to subordinates. Made solicitations. Made sexual requests. Demanded sexual compliance? All of that and more."

He chuckled but it was humorless. "He really is an over achiever, isn't he? And the best part is, we have witness and accusers from this very hospital," he paused. "He assaulted my client in a sexual manner in your facility. We'll be filing a police report on that, by the way. We have testimony that individuals at this hospital requested HR intervention to make the behavior stop. You have policies in place that you have ignored, and that constitutes unlawful conduct. The actions of Billingsly were detestable, but your attempts to cover-up or ignore his unlawful behavior is atrocious and you should be ashamed."

Kate glanced around the room. Some administrators looked shaken; others, defiant.

Here Alec paused, then dropped his other bombshell. "You knowingly hired someone with a history of validated complaints and who had been disciplined and fired for his harassing behavior not only at one previous hospital, but several. This man is a serial offender, and you welcomed him with open arms. Your human resources department tried to intimidate the employees who came to you for redress. Without much effort, we could present a case that will send a message to other hospitals and healthcare institutions that this type of behavior will not be ignored or tolerated. No one should have to endure this manner of degradation in the workplace."

"Now, I don't want to put this nice little community hospital out of business with the kind of judgment I could get from a case like this. I really don't. And your nurse here," he indicated Kate with a wave of his hand, "certainly doesn't. Ms. Gibson was born in this hospital. Her mother trusted the doctors here when she had cancer. The town needs this hospital. *She* has some loyalty." Alec stopped and let his gaze rest on each and every person in the room, save Kate. Most could not meet his eyes. "So this is a warning, ladies and gentlemen, that you had better clean house and clean it well, or we *will* put you out of business."

The hospital attorney cleared his throat. "Mr. Sawyer, Ms. Gibson, please rest assured that we are doing everything in our power to investigate this situation. We're as concerned as you are."

After the meeting, Kate watched the hospital attorney pull Alec aside. The two men conferred and Alec gave a short nod, gathered up his papers and stuffed them into his briefcase. Turning his back on the occupants of the room, he walked over to Kate and ushered her out of the room with a hand at her back.

"Ready?"

"Uh, sure." Kate replied.

"Don't worry, babe. It's all under control," he said in her ear, steering her out to the parking lot.

"Oh. That's a relief."

"Next stop, police station and restraining order."

"Ugh."

He gave her a quick kiss and hustled her into his car.

"Should we stop for a late lunch after?"

"I'd love that. Anywhere but Chez Henri."

He grinned and started the engine.

Alec had called the police station, and Lieutenant Stevenson had an interview room ready for them as soon as they arrived.

"So you guys are an item?" he asked, with a nod to their joined hands.

Her heart gave a little leap and she smiled. "Yep."

He frowned. "Were you together that day on the beach?"

Alec shook his head. "No, we met there."

The lieutenant gave a low whistle. "No kidding. Not the most auspicious beginning."

Alec shrugged. Kate's lips twitched.

Another officer arrived and they began the interview. She ran through the series of events from the first time she met Billingsly to the incident in the supply closet, the pleading text messages and voicemails, the flowers. It was hard to remember all the times and places she'd seen his car, but she did her best. Alec pushed for and got the restraining order.

Lieutenant Stevenson leaned back in the chair. "With cases like these, as your boyfriend has probably told you, it doesn't pay to engage the man."

Kate nodded.

"If he comes within one hundred yards of you, call nine-one-one."

"Got it."

He shot a shrewd look at Alec. "Same goes for you. Don't get into it with him. That's what we're here for."

Alec gave him a wave of acknowledgement, expression grim.

The Chief of Police opened the door and walked into the room. He greeted Kate and Alec and sat down. He took a moment to review the notes the Lieutenant had made. Then he reached across the table and took Kate's hand.

"I want you to know we'll do whatever we have to do to take care of you, Kate. Just like we did with your mother."

Kate looked down, fighting tears. Alec found her hand under the table and gave it a squeeze.

"I know, thanks, Chief." Kate sighed. "I hate to bring this up, given all the trouble we're putting you to with Billingsly, but I should warn you. My sister invited Matt Gibson to spend the holidays with us here in Cielito."

He blanched. "My God."

Kate pressed her lips together. "I know."

He gave Kate a hard look. "Then she can't possibly know—"

Kate interrupted him with a meaningful glance at the Lieutenant, "No. She doesn't. The fewer people who know about *that,* the better. I just wanted to give you guys a heads up."

The Chief shook his head. "I guess I can understand why you wouldn't want to tell her, but he's a manipulative son-of-a-bitch, Kate. Try to nip that in the bud."

"We are," Alec said.

"I'll have my men keep an eye on him once he arrives."

They got back to the car, and Kate's stomach rumbled. He looked over and laughed. "Hungry?"

"Let's just grab burritos and bring them home."

"Do you have a favorite place?"

"There's a great taqueria on Main."

"I know the place." Alec steered the car out of the police station onto the quiet street.

"Alec?"

"Yeah, babe?"

"Why me?"

"Why you?"

"Why is Billingsly interested in me? I mean, we went on this date where he spent the whole time looking at his phone, basically ignoring me, and suddenly he can't leave me alone? It doesn't make any sense."

He reached across and gave her hand a quick squeeze before he had to shift gears again. "I don't have an answer for that. I can tell you that I've been affected by stalkers both personally and professionally. They may look all right on the outside, but inside they're pretty unbalanced individuals."

"But he's a brilliant surgeon. Successful. He's not a madman."

"No." He shrugged. "He probably can't stand to be rejected. At least that's the impression I get from everything you've told me about his past, his reaction to you leaving him at the restaurant, the texts. I'm no psychologist, but from what I understand, stalkers are often intelligent, vengeful, obsessive narcissists. Those characteristics don't preclude him being a successful surgeon. Clearly, you're not the first person to suffer his attentions, but hopefully you'll be the last."

She compressed her lips and looked out the window, trying to stem the flow of tears.

"Kate?"

Alec cursed softly and pulled off onto a side street within walking distance of the restaurant.

He reached for her, she leaned away.

"I hate this. I hate that you have to do all this stuff for me," she wailed. "We just got back together and you have all of my crap to deal with—"

"I love you, Kate. It doesn't matter. Look at me."

Dashing tears away, she turned toward him.

"You know what? I hate that you have to deal with this too, but I love that I'm able to help. And I'm not flailing around wondering how to protect you, Kate. Thanks to my job the last few years, I know how to help, and I'm grateful for that. I want to take care of you. It won't always be like this. I promise."

He got out and walked around the car, opened her door, guided her out, closed and locked it. He hauled her into his strong embrace there on the sidewalk. He held her, just held her until she let herself relax in his arms.

Chapter 24

"Alec?" Kate searched his kitchen for the key ring for the Jonnards' house. Where had she put them? Oh, right. Her purse.

"Babe?" She hollered again. No reply. Hadn't he said he might spend time in the studio this morning? Loathe to disturb him, she wrote a note and left it on the kitchen table.

This was the third time in two days she'd gotten a call from the security company about the damn house. The alarm was having some kind of issue. The police had to deal with it yesterday and last night when she'd been working. If they got dispatched out again, the county policy was to bill her for their time. That she did not need. Kate grabbed her cell phone and dialed the non-emergency police number.

The dispatcher answered. "Cielito Police and Fire."

"Hi, this is Kate Gibson. I'm calling about the alarm you guys are getting on Luna Drive? I'm taking care of it. If it's been dispatched, please cancel it."

"You all are having some issues over there, huh?"

"Yeah. The company is coming out tomorrow to deal with it. If it goes off again, do me a favor and call me first? We can't afford to get a bill from the county."

"No problem. Kate, right? And this is a good number, the one you're calling from?"

"Yeah. Thanks."

There had been no sign of her sister or Matt Gibson yesterday when she'd met the police to check the alarm. From her brief texts with Emma, Kate was pretty sure they arrived and were staying at the cottage. Maybe she would get lucky and catch Emma alone today. This alarm issue gave her a good excuse to go over there.

She parked in the driveway. The car Emma was borrowing from the Morgans wasn't there.

Kate let herself into the main house, she checked the first floor, then wandered up the stairs to check the bedrooms on the second floor. Her nose twitched. It usually smelled musty inside, but today there was another odor. One she couldn't place. Not unpleasant, just unfamiliar. Maybe she'd get the cleaning service back in here. With a shrug, she reset the alarm and let herself out of the house, locking the door behind her.

She turned right into Craig Billingsly.

A furious Craig Billingsly.

Her heart leaped into her throat. She put her arms up defensively.

"You little bitch," he hissed. "I thought you were different. Who do you think you are complaining about me? Getting your boyfriend to get me fired?" He grabbed her by the arms and shook her, hard.

She swung her ring of keys up and managed to catch him in the chin. The keys fell.

"*Hey.*"

Billingsly turned to look at the new arrival a few feet away.

Kate stared. *Is that my father?*

"What the fuck do you think you're doing?"

That *must* be Matt.

The man grabbed Billingsly's shoulder and yanked him off the steps and into the driveway.

"Who the hell are you?"

"Her dad."

"That slut got me fired," Billingsly roared, taking a swing at Matt. Matt deflected the swing, and somehow used the punch to catch the other man off balance. Kate watched her dad send Billingsly sailing to land on all fours on the driveway with a yelp of pain.

Billingsly slowly got up, cradling his hands. "How dare you."

Matt moved forward menacingly. Billingsly raced down the driveway, toward his red Mercedes parked along the curb.

"Come back and you'll regret it," Matt called after him.

He turned to face her and shook his head.

"Friend of yours?" he asked, mockingly.

Her stomach heaved. Here she was, face to face with her mother's abuser. No, her rapist. "No."

Matt Gibson gave her a level look "You got him fired?"

"It's really none of your business." The adrenaline was dissipating and nausea rose up.

His hazel gaze narrowed, lips thinned. "Has he hurt you before?"

Kate frowned. Really? This man, *this man* was offended by physical abuse? If she didn't know what she knew she might buy into his act, the way Emma obviously had. Nope. Rescuing her from Craig Billingsly didn't change anything.

"What do you want?"

He smiled, but it was unpleasant. "To have a nice Thanksgiving with my daughters."

They turned at the sound of a car pulling into the driveway.

Kate left Matt to stride over to the driver's side of the car.

She tried to force the quaver from her voice. "Em?"

Emma avoided eye contact as she got out of the car. "Hey, Kate." She looked past Kate and gave Matt a huge smile. "Dad."

"Let me help you unload the groceries," he said.

Emma tossed him the keys, then turned to Kate. Flipping her hair, she narrowed her eyes. "What brings you here?"

"The alarm in the main house has been malfunctioning."

"Oh."

Matt pulled a grocery bag out of the back seat. "That, and angry ex-boyfriends."

Emma gasped. "What?"

"Craig Billingsly was here, mad of course; the hospital fired him and—"

"*Oh, Kate.*" There was genuine concern on Emma's face. "Are you okay? What happened?"

Matt answered quickly, "He was starting to rough her up, but I put him in his place."

Emma drew in a quick breath. Kate gave him a dirty look over her shoulder.

"Are you all right, Kate?"

"I'm fine."

Emma looked her up and down, then turned to Matt. "And you, Dad?"

"I'm fine, sweetheart. We handled it man to man. He won't be bothering your sister again."

Kate gritted her teeth. Taking a step forward she held out her hand "Emma—"

"You should go, Kate. We have a lot to get done before tomorrow. I'm making a couple of sides."

Kate stood and bit her lip. Matt had already moved up the path to the cottage.

"See? See what a good guy he is? Geez, Kate. You never could stand to be wrong. Why do you have to be so stubborn? He loves us," Emma hissed.

"Has he returned the money yet?" She regretted the words as soon as they were out of her mouth. Emma's face hardened, and she scooted around the car taking an armful of groceries from the trunk.

"Leave, Kate. If it was up to me, I'd have Thanksgiving here with just Dad. He's the one who wants to see you and Alec. God knows why. If you're mean to him tomorrow, we'll go."

Kate watched her retreating back, lips twisting. Damn Emma and damn Billingsly for making Matt look like a hero.

She climbed into her car and set out for the police station.

A few minutes later, Kate parked on the street near the white stucco county building that housed the police department and jail. She sent Alec a brief text, letting him know where she was and why.

Taking a deep breath, she got out of the car, locked it, and marched down the side walk and up the steps.

Kate put her shoulders back and walked over to the young male officer manning the front desk.

"Hi there. I'm Kate Gibson."

"Hi." The uniformed man replied, giving her the once-over, his smile appreciative.

"Is Lieutenant Stevenson in?"

"No, he's out on a call. Something I can help you with?"

Kate bit her lip.

"Kate."

She looked up to see the chief of police heading down the hall toward her.

"Hiya, Chief."

He examined her, his gaze shrewd. "What's happened?"

"Billingsly caught up with me at the Jonnard's when I was there checking out a security alarm."

The chief stood up straighter. "Get Stevenson on the radio." He barked to the officer at the desk. "Are you all right?"

Kate nodded, glancing at her arms. The area where he'd grabbed her was red. With her fair skin, she'd have fingertip-shaped bruises in no time. "Craig shook me. Matt was there and stepped in to defend me."

The chief's eyes bulged. He made a sound between a snort and a grunt.

"Good. Then we have a witness."

"Oh, yeah. Matt saw the whole thing."

"I'll interview you, send Stevenson out to interview your father. On second thought, I'll interview you and then your dad, while my officers look for Billingsly. We'll be able to lock him up. I'll make sure the DA sets the bail high enough that he's not able to get out." He looked at the officer across the desk and jerked his head in Kate's direction. "Did you get all that?"

"Yes, sir."

Kate uttered a small sigh of relief. The holidays would be better if Billingsly was safely locked up.

The chief took her arm and escorted her to his office.

Five minutes later, Alec burst through the door.

The chief's eyebrows vanished into his hairline.

"Kate." He reached out and took her out of the chair into a rough embrace. Then just as quickly, leaned away, examining her carefully.

"Are you all right?" Alec asked.

Heat rose up, sweeping her neck and into her cheeks under the watchful gaze of the chief. "I'm fine, Alec."

Alec looked over to the chief. "What do you need?"

The other man tilted his head and stood. "I've taken her statement. Now I'm going to take Matt Gibson's—"

Alec's shoulders went back and he took a step forward. "You need to pick up Billingsly."

"I have officers on that, young man."

Alec visibly relaxed. "Then I'm taking her home."

The chief's lips quirked. "I was just going to recommend that very thing."

Chapter 25

Thanksgiving morning, Alec adjusted the station on the stereo in his living room, coffee in hand. He and Kate were battling over the music this morning. She kept putting on Christmas music. Thanksgiving was too damn early for Christmas music. His cell rang. It was about time his investigator called.

"Whatcha got?"

"Nothing good, man. This dude is bad news."

"Yeah?" He gave a short laugh. "I'm gonna need more than that to cover your grand a day plus expenses."

The man chortled, a noise that turned into the cough of a chronic smoker.

"I'll send the report, but you said urgent, so I've got some information for you."

While the man briefed Alec, Kate entered the room. She hugged him from behind, resting her cheek on his back.

He pulled her around and held her to the front of his body.

She looked up with a frown and nodded toward the stereo.

"Send me the full report. Okay?" Alec said into the phone.

"I'm pretty sure you want this info—"

"Yeah, yeah, just send it to me."

"I'm not getting great reception—"

"You'll figure it out. And thanks for doing this."

"No problem."

He disconnected the call.

"Alec, the chief just called. They picked up Billingsly in San Diego," Kate said.

"Great."

By mid-morning, Kate was a wreck despite his best efforts to soothe her. He joined her in the kitchen.

Now that Alec and Kate were together, her father would be constantly trying to get into their lives and extort money. He knew it, he accepted it. He had a lot of experience dealing with men like Matt Gibson. Every other musician he dealt with seemed to encounter some kind of blackmailer or extortionist at some point in their career. It was familiar territory.

One way to get the man out of their lives was to pay him. Trouble was, guys like Matt never just had one score. Alec had learned that as soon as he became a successful musician. Instead, they would be back again and again and with more threats. He always recommended against payoffs. Once a client went down that road, it never ended.

Emma and Matt were expected around noon for turkey and all the trimmings. Alec's efforts to bring in a catered meal had been met with patent disbelief a few days earlier. Apparently Kate *always* prepared and cooked the turkey. And Emma always made a few sides. That's the way the Gibsons did Thanksgiving. Diana usually made a few desserts, Kate had said, giving him a meaningful look.

Alec surprised himself by offering to make a pumpkin pie, thus marking his foray into dessert making, or cooking of any kind, for that matter. He was domesticated.

He gave a short laugh.

"What's funny?" Kate looked over at him from her spot by the oven.

"You. Domesticating me," he replied, still grinning and eyeing his pie with pleasure where it sat on the counter, awaiting Cool Whip.

"Oh, that." She gave him an answering smile. "Hey, do you have a carving knife?"

"I'm sure I do…"

"An electric carver?"

"Nah." Alec rifled through the drawers, bringing out a plastic sealed package "I have this baby. Never used it."

"Geez. What *is* that? Looks like something the SEALS would use!"

He read from the packaging. "Says here it's the King of the Kitchen Knife."

She rolled her eyes. "Yes, but will it carve turkey?"

"Nine inches, baby. The king carves up anything."

She laughed.

He put the knife down and fit the front of his body to the back of hers. "I've got your blade right here…" He pushed against her.

She laughed again and butted him away. "Go away, King, Master, whatever, I'm busy. Open that thing for me and leave it on the island, then I have something else for you to do."

She glanced back from where she was basting the turkey and quirked an eyebrow.

Alec laid a loving hand on her back. He would never get tired of her beautiful shape. He looked down at himself ruefully. Amazing. She could turn him on with just a few minutes of horseplay. She glanced at the front of his jeans and giggled.

Alec knew the normalcy wouldn't last; her body had been stiff with tension and anxiety most of the morning. Damn Emma, anyway.

He'd had to talk Kate out of going to her house to check on Emma on an hourly basis yesterday. And since her encounter with Matt yesterday, she'd waffled between feelings of rage toward Matt and fear for Emma. He hadn't seen the need to add additional worry to her plate, but he had similar concerns. In the meantime he was willing to let it play out.

When the doorbell rang close to noon, Kate jumped. Alec gave her a long look.

"I'm fine," she said, smoothing her hair with shaking hands.

He watched her take a deep breath and bite her lip, before meeting his eyes.

"Yeah, right." He opened the door, Kate on his heels.

Zack leapt around them. Alec's smile died when he saw Emma, pale and shaking, eyes swollen, struggling to keep the facsimile of a smile on her face and the containers in her hands from tipping.

Matt stood behind her, eyes glittering with malice and something else: intoxication? It was hard to tell. Though he had seen pictures, he was a bit taken aback by the man's resemblance to Kate and Emma.

The introductions completed, Alec invited them in, nose twitching. Someone had been drinking early or late, or both.

Zack seemed to take an immediate dislike to Matt. He growled and Matt made a kicking motion with his foot.

"Kate," Alec said, evenly. "Can you please put Zack on the patio?"

Kate did as he asked, wordlessly leading the dog by his collar.

"Emma, let me take that from you."

Emma and Matt stepped in and Alec took two Tupperware containers from her trembling hands. Matt held up a plastic bag with bottles of what looked like booze.

"Anyone for a drink?" Matt asked, giving Alec a nasty grin. Alec ignored him, turned and headed down the hall and took the food to the kitchen.

"So. Nice place. Very nice place. What's a place like this worth nowadays?" Matt asked.

Alec had no doubt Matt knew the history of the house, including what he paid for it, annual taxes, and what it was currently worth. Inwardly rolling his eyes, he made a noncommittal response about the housing market in the area.

"Why don't you pour a drink and take it into the living room?" Alec suggested. "Kate and I have a few last minute things to get out of the way, then we'll join you."

They had barely left the room when Kate hissed, furious, "Alec, she's—" He covered her lips with a finger.

"Babe. I know she's really upset. Obviously something happened. If it was bad enough, she would've called or texted.

He's started to show her what a slime he is. Don't give her the opportunity to defend him. We need to let this play out, so she can see what he's like."

Kate's shoulders slumped and her eyes wrinkled at the corners.

"Buck up, love." He squeezed her hand. "I'd give anything to protect you from all of this, but I can't. If we're going to be rid of him, we need him to show Emma his true colors."

"I hate him," she whispered.

He drew her to him.

His phone vibrated in his pocket. He took it out and glanced at the screen. Finally, the email from his investigator. Excusing himself, he walked to the far corner of the kitchen and examined the message. Then read it again.

His investigator had discovered an outstanding felony warrant for Matt Gibson. It was serious enough to have him extradited back to Nevada. No wonder he had come for a visit; things were too hot for him at home. Call the Cielito police now or later? If he called now, given how Matt had rescued Kate the day before, Emma might blame them. It was a tough decision, but he was leaning toward giving the police a heads up a little later.

While the three of them drank iced tea, ate appetizers, and watched football, Matt put down the bourbon like it was last call. His urbane exterior developed significant cracks as he steadily consumed alcohol.

"So, Kate, why didn't you contact me when your mother died?" Matt asked, his smile acid.

"It never entered my mind."

"I'm sure Marilyn gave you an earful about me."

Kate's body stiffened. He gave her knee a squeeze, watching Matt carefully.

The alcohol was making Matt more aggressive by the minute.

Alec watched Kate struggle valiantly with her temper. "Actually, Matt, she never said anything about you."

"You're lying!" he roared.

Emma and Kate jumped.

Alec intervened. "Matt, stop baiting them."

He turned an ugly look on Alec. "Screw you. Speaking of screwing, what's a man of your age doing with my little girl? It's obscene."

Emma flushed.

He didn't think Kate's body could become any more brittle, but it did.

"Hardly," Alec replied, mildly.

Emma stood. "I'm going to the bathroom."

"Let me show you where it is." Kate leaped to her feet.

"Yes, please."

Matt gave Emma a suspicious, narrow-eyed look.

Alec watched the two women walk out of the living room.

*

Kate led the way to the bathroom, stopping just outside. Emma grabbed her arm, tugged her inside and locked the door.

Emma collapsed on the toilet, her large hazel eyes haunted.

"Oh, Kate," she moaned.

Kate crouched in front of her, holding her hands. "What on earth is going on?"

Emma burst into noisy sobs.

"Shhhh." She knelt and patted her sister's back, gently. "Just tell me."

"Kate, I, he's…he's stealing from the main house."

Kate looked at her, brows knitted together. "Come again?"

"He's stealing." She took a gasping breath. "I don't know how many times he's been in there, or why the alarm isn't triggering."

Kate's eyes widened. "My God." She fell back on her heels, stunned.

"I went in his room, your room, while he was showering this morning. I…I was just going to see if he had any dirty laundry in his bag and wash it for him…and I saw a bunch of things, Kate. He's got all these black duffel bags, filled with silver and other stuff." Her voice rose. "You know that sports memorabilia collection Mr. Jonnard had in the study? Most of it was in a duffel bag. There were frames and…and…I.. I don't know how he could've gotten it, Kate, but inside his suitcase I found your ring of keys—"

Kate covered her mouth with her hand. "Oh, no." She had forgotten all about dropping that ring of keys in the confrontation with Billingsly. She smacked her head. Some of the safe keys were on there, locked up electronic devices, some costume jewelry—which for wealthy people like Mrs. Jonnard—could mean a lot of gold and silver. And she was supposed to be the caretaker.

Kate searched her pockets for her phone. Damn it. She'd left it in the kitchen.

"Have you got your phone?"

"Mine's in my purse, in the foyer."

Taking a deep breath, Kate wrapped Emma up in her arms.

"Kate, I'm so sorry, the money, everything—"

"Shhhh. It's okay. Listen, we need to keep this on the down low until I can get to my phone or tell Alec. Can you relax a bit?"

Emma dashed away tears. "I can try."

"Let's get your phone."

Emma led the way out to the living room. Kate pasted on a smile.

"What's going on?" Matt asked, glancing between the two women.

"Nothing," Emma replied, too quickly.

Matt's eyes narrowed further. His shrewd gaze bore into Kate. He stood unsteadily.

Alec came in from the kitchen and moved to where the women stood, frozen.

"What's going on?" Alec asked. "Emma?"

Emma burst into noisy sobs. "I want him to leave."

"Time to go, Matt," Alec said.

Matt smiled. "How 'bout you make me leave? Permanently."

Kate's mouth dropped open.

"That didn't take long, Matt. Let me guess, I'm supposed to give you money so you leave the girls alone?" Alec said.

"I know what you're worth. You won't even miss it," Matt replied.

Kate gasped, outraged, turning to face Alec. His expression was unchanged.

He's been expecting this. Nausea moved through Kate. She put a hand to her stomach. It wasn't fair. First his family, now hers? She'd be damned if she'd let him.

Shaking, Kate turned to him. "Alec. If you care for me you will not pay that bastard one red cent. He's already taken enough from us."

Alec gave her a reassuring smile. "It's not that I'm morally opposed to paying to have trash taken away from my home. The problem I have is that the trash never goes away permanently."

Matt tried to interrupt but Alec talked over him, studying his nails.

"So I'm going to tell you no. Not a dime."

Kate hugged Emma to her and held her.

"Ladies, why don't you go to the kitchen?" Alec suggested. The two women moved behind Alec.

"I wish I'd never met you." Emma sobbed, facing her dad. "You're nothing but a thief."

Matt's eyes widened and the mask fell away. His face twisted in fury.

Kate instinctively stepped closer to Alec, pulling Emma behind her and away from their father.

"A thief?" Alec asked. "Kate?"

Kate sighed. So much for keeping that on the down low. "He's been stealing from the Jonnards."

"I'm calling the police." Alec drew his phone from his pocket then herded the two women into the kitchen.

Kate turned, startled by the *thwunk* behind her and just in time to see Alec crumple to the ground. Emma screamed. Matt approached his prone body, long, heavy, pewter vase in hand. Yellow tulips and water spread over the hardwood floor.

"Emma. Get your phone. Call nine-one-one," Kate instructed softly, giving her a shove toward the direction of the front door, inching toward her father.

Matt bent and raised the vase in the air, ready to administer another blow.

Kate dove for him. The impact knocked them both to the hardwood floor, the vase fell to the ground. Grunting, they wrestled near the fireplace. Kate was vaguely aware of someone screaming. Short bursts of hysteria, punctuated by her pants and Matt's snarling. Matt threw an elbow. The blow connected with her cheek and eye. Her head snapped back and she saw stars for a moment.

Pain turned to rage in an instant. As he struggled to get purchase on her, she sank her teeth into the nearest part of her father's anatomy. His bicep. Matt shook her off with a howl, and scrambled away. She crawled after him and he kicked at her, catching her in the shoulder. She flew back with a grunt of pain.

Matt got to his feet and lurched toward the kitchen. Her father, not completely sober or sane. Heading into the kitchen. Her brain pieced things together with startling awareness, the carving knife on the counter. Every impulse narrowed and focused.

Kate picked up the heavy, wet vase lying next to Alec's body. Her left arm was not responding to the commands her brain was sending. Dislocated, she noted dispassionately.

Alec was moaning now, though it was hard to hear him over Emma's hysterical sobs. She didn't give them a thought as she followed Matt, moving deliberately toward the kitchen. Kate could only see out of one eye, the other nearly swollen shut. Holding the heavy vase behind her, she entered the kitchen.

Chapter 26

Kate stood in the entryway, watching silently as Matt picked up the carving knife laid out on the island. If he wanted to get to Emma or Alec, he would have to go through her. Sensing her presence, he whirled, knife in hand, raised it as he lunged toward her.

"Screw you and your rich boyfriend!" he screamed, his face a mottled mask of rage.

She waited until the last second, hampered by her impaired vision, then swung with every ounce of strength. The heavy vase connected with his arm, releasing a loud crack. Matt howled in pain, dropped the knife and cradled his injured arm to his body, backing up. She kicked the knife away. It skittered across the floor. She advanced on him, vase held high. Her heart raced fury through her veins. He held up his good arm to ward her off, cringing. She moved forward, tightening her grip on the vase, eager to keep swinging.

"Kate," Alec's slurred voice came from behind her. "Kate."

She stiffened, but she didn't dare look at him. She didn't dare take her good eye off her father.

Matt heard him. His eyes were wild.

"I'm gonna sit here—" Alec said weakly, from behind her. She heard him hit the floor, not gracefully. Her anger abated. The sound of sirens was drawing closer.

"Emma!"

"I'm here." Her voice quavered from the entryway.

"Make sure Alec stays down. Let the police in when they come."

*

Alec heard himself moan.

Oh no.

Had he been using again? He had the mother of all hangovers. He didn't dare open his eyes. The pain in his head was a relentless, piercing agony. He opened one eye carefully, groaning at the fresh wave of pain and nausea. A face loomed over him. Who was that? He couldn't place the man.

"God," he groaned. "What happened?" He was slurring. Was he wasted? Not around Kate. Please, anything but that. Another face and torso with a uniform came into view. This one he didn't recognize.

The room was spinning, the pain in his head incapacitating. He closed his eyes and had a very real fear that he would throw up, lying on his back. Was that to be his fate? Kinda cliché for a rock musician.

"Babe, you going to get sick?" Kate asked him. It was Kate, all right. Her scent, the sound of her voice was unmistakable. She was here? Witnessing this?

"Nah." He didn't have a clue how he came to be lying here on his back, but he'd be damned if he'd get sick in front of her. He was vaguely aware of radios squawking, and lots and lots of male voices.

"A precaution, Mr. Sawyer." He tried to open his eyes, but the pain was worse that way. Someone put something stiff and plastic around his neck. An immobilization device. He felt himself lifted onto something. Even that small amount of movement had him groaning. He felt a hand take his. Kate. Even in his agony, he knew her touch.

"S'all right, Kate," he slurred as they moved him again, up in the air, then rolled him gently. "I'll fix this."

"There's nothing to fix, Alec. Everything's under control. The medics are taking you to the hospital for evaluation. It's just a precaution. You might have a concussion."

Kate sounded…neutral. He didn't think he'd ever heard her use that distant, professional voice before.

Ah. So he hadn't been drinking. Despite the pain, a wave of relief washed over him. Thank God.

Alec lay there holding her hand. He gave a squeeze to let her know he'd heard her. More movement, shuffling him around. It hurt to breathe.

*

Kate let go of Alec as they lifted him from the backboard onto the stretcher near the front door. "How's he doing?" Emma asked.

"They'll put him in the ambulance for transport. They might try to start an IV before heading out," Kate replied, dully. Her gut churned in earnest and she forced down nausea. Lightheaded, she sat down abruptly on the tile floor. Then the shaking started. She shook so hard her teeth chattered. She put her head in her hand, the other arm hanging useless.

"Oh God. Oh God."

She realized, distantly, that she was on the verge of hysteria.

Emma knelt next to her, holding her good side.

"Kate. Calm down. Kate, he's okay. He's going to be okay." Emma kept repeating the words over and over.

Kate turned to look at her. Emma cast a worried glance at the police officer who was watching their interaction closely. The man waved the ambulance crew over to Kate. They checked her eye, gave her an ice pack, took her vitals and examined her shoulder. She flinched away. They made quick work of immobilizing it in a sling. She couldn't concentrate on what was being said. Nothing made sense.

There was a keening noise in the distance. Emma's hands turned her face roughly. Their eyes met.

"Kate. Stop it." Emma's voice was stern, almost angry. "He's okay. He's going to be okay. He's talking. He probably just got a concussion. Nod if you understand me."

Kate nodded and dissolved in sobs.

"They want to take you in. They're worried about a possible concussion because of your eye. They also want to check your shoulder." Emma's voice was calm and patient.

Kate nodded. "I'm riding with Alec." She made a superhuman effort to get her emotions under control and stand up.

"I don't think they want …" Emma's voice trailed off at the expression in Kate's good eye. Emma reached to gently aide her sister to her feet.

"I'll tell them," Emma agreed, hastily.

The medics helped Kate into the back of the ambulance where she buckled herself in on the bench next to Alec. She held his hand all the way to the hospital.

An hour later, she sat in a chair in the behind the curtain in the empty emergency room cubicle, waiting for Alec to get back from his CAT scan.

Nothing functioned properly, not her body, numb and spent, not her shoulder—immobilized by a sling—and not her vision, one eye still swollen shut. Her thoughts were stuck in a continuous sluggish loop, reliving what had happened in Alec's living room, in his kitchen.

Her father tried to kill Alec. Tried to kill her. She hadn't thought him capable of it. Underestimating Matt Gibson was a mistake, and one she would never make again. Her first order of business would be to get Alec out of her life. She could not allow him to be drawn in to her messed up family. He'd fought enough of her battles. And look where it had gotten him. Kate and Emma would never be rid of Matt. Her father's attempt to extort money from Alec rang in her ears. Matt would be incarcerated long enough to keep him away from Emma's college tuition money, but long term? No.

The idea of letting Alec go had grief clawing her insides, a howling thing desperate to get out. She buried it.

Alec's family had tried to steal from him and hadn't bothered to step in when he was killing himself with drugs and alcohol. He didn't need to be involved with a woman whose father was not only a rapist but a murderer. Her dad made his parents look saintly. If he wasn't in her life, he couldn't be affected. Simple.

Alec's recently revamped image would come under fire when this story got out. And it would. Of that she had no doubt. People were already talking; she could hear them whispering about her and Alec and Matt.

Matt was currently chained to a gurney in the emergency room with a passel of police guarding him. Doubtless they would get the details of this Thanksgiving fiasco wrong, and Alec would end up the bad guy. She could picture the headlines "Alec Sawyer Hospitalized After Thanksgiving Day Drunken Brawl".

This time when nausea threatened, she found herself on her knees in front of the biohazard trash receptacle, retching. When her stomach was empty, she sat back on her heels, sweating and shaking.

One of the emergency room doctors entered the room. She paused in front of Kate and gently helped her back into the chair. Pulling out her pen light, she checked Kate's pupils.

The doctor disappeared only to return with a cola moments later. She opened it and put it in Kate's palm. Then with a shake of her head, put the ice pack into Kate's unresisting fingers and moved it to her face.

"Keep it on your eye." She stroked Kate's hair a moment, before she slipped back out through the curtain. Kate looked up; she hadn't even had the wherewithal to thank her.

The doctor had repositioned her arm when she first arrived. The sharp pain of the maneuver that put the joint back in had been replaced by a throbbing ache. Good. She could focus on that pain instead of her heartache. Absently, she adjusted the ice pack on her shoulder.

Emma was out of the way. She hadn't put up much resistance when Kate insisted that she go with their family friends the Morgans. Roy promised he would run Emma by the police station for a statement. He assured her he would to try to salvage what remained of Thanksgiving. The police had been kind enough to interview Kate during Alec's examination.

The loss of consciousness and severity of the concussion meant an overnight stay for Alec. She'd be damned if she'd leave him alone.

She took Alec's phone from the bedside tray and called Dave. She filled him in on the day's events in a monotone. He wanted to come up immediately, but she forestalled him.

"Enjoy your day with your family. I'll stay with him tonight. Can you pick him up and take him to Los Angeles tomorrow? He's going to need a few days of enforced rest."

There was silence on the other end.

"So, I'm the enforcer, am I? Where will you be?" Dave responded, a wealth of kindness in his voice.

Her teeth clenched as another wave of grief crested, washing over her. She waited for it to pass. It didn't. "Here," she managed.

"I think he'd rather you took care of him," he said softly. "And I'm thrilled to hand off that responsibility to you."

She didn't trust her voice and tears welled in her eyes.

"Are you there?" Dave asked.

"Trust me, Dave; he's better off without me and my psycho father."

"The Alec I know is more than capable of handling someone's daddy issues. Don't underestimate him."

"I've made up my mind."

"Kate, please don't do this. You're the best thing that ever happened to Alec, and he knows it."

"I have all your contact info in my phone. I'll text you the specifics for tomorrow. The nurse will give you the discharge instructions," she replied and hung up.

*

Alec had a private room but try as he might he couldn't get Kate to lie down and rest with him. He knew something was wrong; her body was rigid when she embraced him. But between the headache, nausea, and a vague sense of confusion he couldn't put two thoughts together. Alec had met with the police twice already, but he wasn't much help. He couldn't remember anything from Thanksgiving morning and didn't remember the fight at all. Instead, there were jumbled memories of pumpkin pie making and Christmas music.

The ride in the ambulance to the hospital was the only memory he had. Normal with a concussion to have some amnesia, he was told. Maybe he'd feel better after sleep. At some point during the night he was restless; Kate woke him gently and crawled into the bed to lie in his arms.

The next morning he felt a hundred times better, but there was no sign of Kate.

Alec narrowed his eyes when Dave walked in. "Where is she?"

Dave lifted his brows. "She didn't say goodbye?"

Alec scowled and swore. His head throbbed angrily in response. He relaxed his brow. Better.

Dave glanced around the room. "This might answer some questions." He grabbed an envelope off the rolling hospital tray.

Alec ripped open the letter, scanned it and snorted. *Ouch.* Damn.

Dave pursed his lips. "I've been talking to the doctors. You need a few quiet days to recover. No theatrics." He took the note back from Alec and studied it.

Alec considered his friend. "A few days." He started to nod, then froze and made a mental note not to move his head. "Yes. That'll work."

"I must say you're handling *this*," Dave shook the note "better than expected."

He gave Dave a hard look. "Burn that."

*

"Dave?" Kate's voice was barely audible. She was trying not to wake Emma sleeping in the next room, so she had called from the bathroom.

"Yes?"

"It's Kate. I wanted to be sure you understood the discharge instructions."

"What discharge instructions?"

"*Dave*," she hissed, "didn't they tell you what to look for? Confusion, vomiting, dizziness, memory problems—"

"I think maybe you'd better come here and take care of him. Sounds like he may need a private nurse."

"Not funny." Her shoulders slumped as the tension left her body. "Don't tease me. Is he okay?"

"Physically? Yes. He's fine, other than some headaches. But Kate—"

"Listen, I gotta run. I wanted to check on him. Don't tell him I called."

Dave grunted.

"Take care of him for me." Her voice broke, and she disconnected the call. She put the phone down on the counter carefully and turned on the shower, barely able to see through the veil of tears, fighting sobs that were sure to wake Emma. Stripping out of her clothes, she entered the shower. Within minutes, she was sitting on the tile, the water poured over her, mingling with her tears.

She stayed there until the water ran cold. She was pruned and shivering but mostly back in control by the time she climbed out. Catching a glance of her reflection in the mirror, she flinched. The black eye was violet and swollen, both eyes bloodshot. Her fair skin was blotchy. She looked like hell and it had only been two days. It would get better. It had to.

Meanwhile, she would stay busy. Kate had a long overdue heart-to-heart last night with a tearful, remorseful Emma. They were slated to have brunch with Ava, then see a movie and avoid the post-Thanksgiving shopping hoards.

Emma had plans with high school friends for dinner that night. Kate would finally get to be alone with her grief.

She would get through this. Tomorrow she would take Emma to LA for her flight back to Washington, D.C.

*

Alec sat on his couch in Los Angeles, flipping through channels, bored silly, when Dave came back into his living room.

He raised an eyebrow and got a nod from Dave.

"Checking up on me?"

Another nod.

Alec grinned. "Should've told her I had a relapse."

Dave put his hands on his hips. "Is that how you want to play it?"

Alec scowled and touched his forehead. "Goddamn headache is still here."

"I overheard you talking to the police yesterday."

"Yeah?"

"Did she really go after her dad after he knocked you out?"

Alec's fists clenched involuntarily. "Apparently."

"Tackled him?"

"Yeah."

"And then approached him while the bloodthirsty son-of-a-bitch still had the knife?"

"That's what the police told me."

Emma and Kate relayed exactly the same story.

"He really was going to kill you."

Alec's reply was terse. "Stupid bastard. Kill the goose with the golden egg? He's smarter than that, but he was pretty enraged and drunk. From what the police tell me, they were closing in on him in Vegas. He was getting desperate. Desperate people—"

Dave waved. "Yeah, yeah, so essentially Kate saved your life."

Alec met his gaze. "No 'essentially' about it, she did."

"And you are going to let her go?" Dave asked, incredulous.

Alec resumed his channel surfing, expressionless.

Dave's cell rang again. Alec grinned watching as Dave recognized the number, and the expression of puzzlement and surprise it generated.

Everything was falling into place.

*

A few hours later, one of the partners at the firm returned his call. "Alec Sawyer."

"Alec, Bill Emery. Listen, I'm sure you know the firm is not thrilled with your recent publicity—"

"Thanks for calling me back. I quit." As soon as he said the words, he felt liberated, truly free for the first time in years.

There was a long period of silence on the other end of the line.

"Sawyer, it's not as bad as it seems. The positive publicity you got from the rescue counteracts this little drunken brawl—"

Alec interrupted. "I'm not quitting because of that. I'm getting back into music. Appreciate the opportunity to work with you all, but it isn't for me. I'll wrap up what I can in the next few weeks and pass off the rest to an associate."

The man on the other end of the phone sighed. "You know, in one way I'm sad to lose you, Sawyer. You worked hard for the firm and were quite the rainmaker…on the other hand, I was a huge fan of Reeking Bliss and am happy to hear you're getting back into the business. If there's ever anything you need—"

"Thanks. There are a couple of issues I'm dealing with, like the attempt on my life you probably read about. If I need help, I'll throw the work your way. There's another issue I want to talk about, and I know you're the best the firm has for this type of work."

Chapter 27

"You okay?" Emma looked over, frowning.

"Totally fine, lost in thought," Kate lied, watching the road carefully. In a few hours she would drop off her sister, and then Emma would be gone until Christmas. Maybe she could pull herself together by then. Right. Like she would ever recover from him. At least Kate wouldn't have to keep pretending everything was fine. Putting on a good front required every ounce of energy she had these days and it still wasn't fooling anyone.

"You did a pretty good job hiding your black eye with makeup." Emma said, looking her over critically.

It had been four days and the swelling had diminished, but the delicate skin around and under the eye was an exotic combination of green and yellow. A few more days and she wouldn't have to look in the mirror and relive that awful scene—the terror as she realized her father was going to kill her unconscious boyfriend, the fight in the kitchen.

The media frenzy had finally abated. The first day or two, paparazzi loitered in front of the hospital, at Alec's beach house, all over Cielito. She could only image how upset he was. God, what a mess. Roy had let her know this morning that Alec was pressing charges against her father. Adding his charges to the ones she already filed would increase the likelihood that Matt Gibson would not make bail. He would go to prison for a long while—or he could be paroled in a few years.

Keeping Alec in her life wasn't worth the risk. Insomnia, grief, and endless bouts of weeping had left her numb. Drained. She'd caught the sympathetic looks from Emma, Roy, Diana, and Ava over the last few days. Ava had made it very clear she didn't accept

Kate's reasons for breaking up with Alec, but once she realized the fragile state Kate was in, she had become silent on the matter.

"Kate," Emma's tone was buoyant. Kate turned to her, recalled from her daze.

"My friend's brother texted me. He's a waiter at this awesome West Hollywood restaurant. I thought it would be cool to go in for lunch before you drop me for my flight. He says he can get us a table. Please?"

"Uh…how come you didn't mention it this morning?" Her hands tensed on the wheel and she shot her sister a glance.

Emma flushed and her eyes darted away.

"Em?"

"I just got the text." Emma sounded defensive.

"Em, I dunno—"

"We were planning to eat in LA anyway. Please Kate?" she begged. "He is *so* fine."

Oy. She was not in the mood. But after all they'd been through the past few days she wasn't going to chance a fight with Emma right before she had to fly back to school. She could tolerate a meal out, couldn't she?

"I guess." Her reply was begrudging.

Emma bounced in her seat.

"I don't want you to miss your flight. You know how L.A. traffic can be." She made a final attempt to change Emma's mind.

"It's not far from the airport," Emma assured her sister breezily. "My phone says we're only thirty minutes away."

Kate found parking easily, locked the car and followed her sister up the street to the restaurant.

"This place?" Kate said in disbelief, standing in front of the entrance. "Even I've heard of this place, Em. It'll be a fortune."

Emma was already craning her neck toward the patio, looking for a hot guy or celebrities or both.

"God help me," Kate whispered, trying to rub away the tension that kinked her neck as she followed her sister into the establishment.

"Hi!" Emma greeted the bombshell hostess. "I'm Emma? For the patio?"

The girl beamed at them. "Follow me," she instructed, leading them through the restaurant. Emma walked as slowly as possible, looking this way and that. She nudged Kate and hissed, "Look."

Kate caught sight of the actor who played the caped crusader on the big screen, sitting at a table with another man, even better looking in real life, if that was possible. She looked away. She didn't want to be caught gawking. Emma seemed to have no trouble with it. She sent a huge smile in his direction. Kate bit back a laugh, the first in days. Emma was her usual irrepressible self. Granted, Kate still had work to do to repair the damage from her half-truths and lies, but the bond was solid; all the truth Emma needed to know about their dad and their finances were out there and for that she was grateful.

At the patio, the hostess led them to an area under big white umbrellas. An area that had been decorated for a party. There were arrangements of white and red flowers, silver streamers and silver and white balloons next to a "Congratulations" sign.

A huge cake with a blue fondant border around each of the four tiers sat in the center of the long table.

"I think there's been some mistake…" her voice trailed off as she caught sight of Ava talking with Dave and his wife under an umbrella.

Kate's heart ceased beating for a moment.

Alec was here, his back to her. He was talking with an older couple.

Kate noticed the older woman's resemblance to Dave. Were they the Thatchers? Her heart picked up its pace at triple speed. She glanced about her in bewilderment and spotted Roy and Diana talking to Asher. He was hard to miss in a tank which revealed his spectacular ink, jeans, and combat boots.

Emma shouted "Hello" to those gathered and continued to pull Kate's resisting body forward.

Everyone on the patio was staring at Kate. She put her hand to her throat as Alec turned and met her gaze. He strode over and she put her arms up. To ward him off? To draw him to her? She didn't know anymore. She'd never been so confused or so vulnerable.

He ignored her arms and gathered up her stiff body. An unnatural hush fell over the patio. Pulling back, Kate looked up at him, memorizing every one of his beloved features. She read intent in the set of his jaw, but there was something desperate in his sky-blue eyes.

"Alec," she said softly.

"Yes, my love?"

She flinched at the endearment.

"What's going on?" Her voice came out a reedy whisper.

There was a flurry of activity outside the fenced patio. She glanced past him to see men with cameras, shouting and lining up at the gated edge of the restaurant patio. Kate turned back to Alec, stunned. The paparazzi? Here?

Alec grinned.

"Did you really think I was going to let you go?" he asked. "Haven't you figured out that you can't protect the ones you love? Or are you trying to protect your own heart? You don't need to protect it from me; I care for it more than my own."

She barely even registered that she was crying. "I love you, Alec, but my father nearly killed you."

"So he did. Nearly being the operative word. Kate, when I told you I love you, I'm not a guy who says that lightly. I'm not sure I believed in love the way I feel it for you. I'm in love with you, Kate. Did you save my life only to leave me miserable without you? Because I won't let you do it."

He slipped a black box from the front pocket of his well-worn jeans and went down on one knee. There was a slight tremor in his hand.

Her fingers went to her mouth, covering it in shock.

"Alec." She found herself caught between laughter and tears. "What are you doing, you lunatic?"

"Will you marry me, Kate? I've invited all our loved ones and some," he gestured to the paparazzi with a tilt of his head "who don't love me so well, to witness this. No pressure though. Take your time."

She leaned over, she didn't have far to bend, and put her heart and soul into the kiss she laid on him.

The kiss got so heated, so fast, Alec dropped the box and crushed her to him, until finally she pulled away, breathless.

There was a collective laugh from the people gathered on the patio, and cat-calls from the paparazzi. Kate blushed, urging Alec to his feet, and he scooped up the box.

She stared at the ridiculously large stone he placed on her finger. She turned it this way and that.

"Like it?" he asked.

She bit back a smile. "It's… obnoxious."

He grinned. "That's *exactly* what I was going for."

"Maybe I could get my forehead tattooed with 'Mrs.' or 'taken' instead?"

"Babe, you get a forehead tattoo and it won't matter what it says, people will stay away."

She sobered. "Alec…" She tried not to cry, she really did, but the tears kept flowing. "I want you to know how much I love you…" Her voice broke on a sob and he hugged her fiercely.

"I do know, Kate," His breath hitched. "But not nearly as much as I love you."

*

Hours later they lay in his big bed, the last rays of the afternoon sun giving the room a soft, romantic feel.

"I quit my job."

Kate bolted upright and half turned to stare at him. "*What?*"

He pulled her back down.

"Quit. Yesterday. I've got a few things to wrap up, but I'm moving on," he stated, calmly.

"To do what?" she interrupted, but he could hear the hope in her voice, she rolled over onto him and peered at him through tangled hair.

He beamed at her and she gave a shout.

"Oh, Alec. I'm so happy."

"Me too, baby."

"Are you sure?"

"As soon as I did it, I knew it was the right thing."

She bounced up and down on him. He laughed. Their laughter turned to kisses and the white hot flare of passion.

An hour later he lay, watching her doze.

Her eyes slowly fluttered open, confusion chased away by dawning awareness, then joy.

"Mmmm." She stretched. "Did I fall asleep?"

They stared at each other across the pillow.

"Tell me everything," she whispered. "Will you go on the road right away?"

He chuckled. "You don't have any idea how it works do you?"

"No clue."

"You ready to hear my plan?"

"Sure."

"I'm starved. Let's order in."

He ordered their dinner while she dressed. He pulled on jeans and they went to curl up on the couch.

"I'm tempted to take you to Las Vegas tonight." He checked her expression.

Amusement warred with horror on her face.

He grinned. "But I've done that. This has to be special. I've had Ava working on the arrangements for a wedding a few days before Christmas."

She nodded, looking slightly crestfallen. "I agree. We'll need a year to plan it if you want a big wedding."

He laughed. "Not next year, in three weeks."

"Alec," she sputtered, spilling tea on herself, and brushing at it ineffectually. "There is no way!"

"Do you want a big wedding?"

"Of course not."

"Me neither. If we have the wedding on the beach, we might have to keep the date a surprise so we don't get inundated, but I figure a small catered reception at my beach house if you want. If that seems like too much, maybe at the country club?"

"I want to get married on the beach where we met in Cielito." she said, dreamily, then sat up. "Alec! I'll need a dress…work, I—"

"You'll have everything you want. And probably stuff you don't, knowing Ava." He laughed. "She's on it." He grasped her chin and pulled her head up until her concerned eyes met his. "If you don't trust me, will you at least trust Ava?"

She smiled. "Okay, Alec. Yes, I trust you and Ava."

"Okay. That's settled. I can work any number of places but I'll be collaborating for some of it, so while I'll be able to do some recording in Cielito, I'll be in L.A. a lot. Are you good with that?"

She bit her lip.

"Talk to me," he said.

"I guess I envisioned us being together, not all the time, but not doing what we've been doing with these long absences. Especially if we're married."

He waited, but she frowned, twirling her hair.

"I've given that a lot of thought. Do you want to know what I've come up with?"

She nodded, meeting his eyes.

"Do you want to keep working?"

She frowned. "Of course, Alec. I'm not going to become your dependent."

He sighed. "I knew you'd feel that way. You don't *need* to work."

"That's not the point."

"I know, but I…I had this idea…"

"Okay…"

"I'd like us to be together, and at some point that will mean travel."

"A hospital nursing schedule is pretty restrictive."

She nodded.

He blew out a breath. "So my firm has set up foundations for some artists. I've been thinking about starting my own. My Reeking Bliss royalties can fund it."

She cocked her head, listening intently.

"Eventually, we might be able to get other people involved, do benefits, that kind of thing. I thought you might be interested in the organizational piece. Maybe bring Ava on to coordinate some events, fundraising."

"What kind of foundation?"

He took a deep breath. "There are all kinds of needs out there, but I can't seem to get your mother out of my mind. Thinking about what she must have gone through. How much worse it could have been for you both if she'd died before you turned eighteen. If she hadn't had a life insurance policy in place. If Roy and Diana were without means…"

Kate stared at him, her hand at her throat, tears trailing down her cheeks.

His own throat thickened and he took her hand.

"Alec, I don't know what to say."

He nodded. "I know nursing is your thing, but--"

"I want to do it," she said, fiercely, wiping at her face. "Of course I want to do it. I can't think of anything more meaningful than helping families with a terminally ill parent."

"I think with your history, it might be better if we went public. Tell your story. I've got some clients with pretty deep pockets who might be interested in contributing. I've done enough research in the last few days to know there is a real need out there. The families need all kinds of support, legal, financial, medical. You name it."

"Oh, Alec." Her hands were clasped together in front of her.

"We can start slow. We'll have to have a system to investigate applicants, but we can work with local hospices and state agencies. We'll need a board, which I can help with, and a team that might include nurses, social workers, physicians and attorneys."

Her eyes were shining, rapt. "Yes. I could coordinate those groups. I've worked with families on end-of-life issues at the hospital. We can do this, Alec."

"I'm pretty excited about it, too, almost as much as the idea of getting back into the studio," he said, grinning. "By the way, I booked Emma on a flight first thing tomorrow."

"Good. Is she coming here later tonight with Ava?"

"No, they figured we could use some privacy."

"Are they staying in a hotel?"

"No. Asher said he'd take them out on the town, and then put them up at his place."

She drew back. "Oh Alec, Asher?" she said with dismay, her hands searching for and finding the locket on her chest.

He grinned and pulled her back down into his arms.

"They'll have fun. He's a good time."

"That's what I'm worried about!"

The End

About the Author

Fueled by black jellybeans and pinot noir—never together—Rachel Cross writes sexy, sweet contemporary romance. She lives by the beach in California with her surfer/ helicopter pilot husband and two daughters. Before becoming a romance author, she was a firefighter, paramedic, clinical research manager, and *Weekly World News* tabloid model. Please visit her website at *www.readrachelcross.com*

A portion of the earnings from *Rock Her* will be donated to local Hospices. Thank you for your purchase and contributing to the care and support of families facing life-limiting illnesses. ,For more information about Hospice, please visit *http://www.nhpco.org/*.

In the mood for more Crimson Romance?
Check out *Seduction's Canvas* by K.M. Jackson at
CrimsonRomance.com.